Mike & Jane

Guess 'whodunit'!

J. H. Clue

7-24-2009

Heb. 4:13

The Pastor & The Private Eye
©2007 by Thomas H. Pine
First Printing, 2007,
ISBN: 0-9722385-2-2
ISBN-13: 978-09722385-2-6
Printed in the United States of America

All characters in this book have no existence outside of the imagination of the author and have no relation whatsoever to anyone bearing the same name or names. They are not even distantly inspired by any individual known or unknown to the author, and all incidents are pure invention.

This edition published by arrangement with Authors Ink Books.

THE PASTOR
&
THE PRIVATE EYE

A CILLA STEPHENSON MYSTERY

T. H. PINE

Burr Oak, Michigan

CHAPTER 1:
ACCUSED!

"You have the right to remain silent...." The words the police officer read off his Miranda card echoed in Vint's ears like a line out of some cop show. Here he was, Vinton "Vint" Montrose, spread out against a police cruiser, his hands being cuffed. How had it come to this? Just yesterday he was the pastor of a small rural church in central Pennsylvania, with all the cares and responsibilities that job entailed. Today, he was the prime suspect in a murder investigation into the death of a young woman from his church. The whole incident was so surreal in Vint's mind it was as though it were happening to another person.

Rebecca "Becky" Langsfelder was a beautiful, vivacious young secretary who worked at the bank in Bronson and attended Vint's church. Vint knew her well, since the young woman harbored a crush on him from the start of his tenure there. This was his first church and, as yet, Vint was unmarried. He expected a bit of female attention, but Becky had set her cap for him and made no bones about it. Now, she was dead — victim of a rape and strangling. Because of Vint's past with Becky, the police suspected him. He had been questioned about two weeks ago, and he told them he had dated her a couple of times, but nothing serious had developed between them. They asked him a lot of embarrassing questions about his relationship with Becky — 'Did you have sex? Did you ever argue? Were you into any kinky stuff? Did you drink a lot when you were together?' — stuff like that. Now, thinking they had enough unanswered questions, they had arrested him.

The police officer bundled Vint into the back of the cruiser. Vint almost grinned when the officer placed his hand on his head and shoved him into the back seat. Vint had seen it a hundred times on the cop shows on TV and in the movies and had always thought it was a little incongruous — cops being so solicitous over some creep hitting his head. Now that it was Vint's head, the irony didn't escape him.

Jim Fournier was a forensic pathologist at the Altoona Morgue. A native of Montreal, he moved to Altoona in response to a job opening report he got over the Internet. Jim wanted to escape the hassle of big city living, so he checked out the setup in Altoona, fell in love with the surrounding rural area, and moved to a small house on three acres. At first he took some ribbing from his Irish and German surnamed coworkers over his French moniker, but that all died down in a short time; Jim was beginning to fit in well. The only part of the job that still bothered him was lying on the autopsy table in front of him.

"The victim is a female Caucasian," he said into the overhead mike, "approximately five-four, one hundred fifteen pounds, with blonde hair and..." he pried open one of her eyes, "... blue eyes. Fournier referred to the clipboard he held in his left hand. "Age, twenty-two years."

Cases like this one always made Jim sad. He looked down at the young woman's nude form on the table, her fair skin showing starkly white under the bright fluorescent lights. She was a pretty little thing, with a near-perfect figure. A small group of three moles on her stomach, under her right breast, gave her a vulnerable look, which was not lost on Jim. She had shaved her pubis for some reason, so she looked even younger than her twenty-two years, almost pre-pubescent. Jim inwardly prayed he would only have sons. He couldn't imagine the depth of grief the parents of this beautiful young woman were experiencing at this moment.

"...The victim appears to had been strangled, with ligature marks around the sides and laryngeal area of the neck, consistent with the use of hands. Individual finger marks are evident. Judging from the size of the marks, the hands appear to be large, thus male. Moving down, there are bruises on both breasts that indicate rough treatment. There also appears to be tooth marks on the nipples. Additional heavy bruising on the lower stomach, mons veneris, and thigh, support the hypothesis that rape is a factor." Jim took a wooden speculum from the tray at the side of the table and inserted it into the girl's vagina. Withdrawing it, he examined the end. "There appears to be no semen present. Residue seems to be normal, vaginal secretions." He placed the speculum in a small plastic bag for lab testing. "There are a large number of small contusions all over the victim's body, so it's possible she was naked for a long time. Additional scrapes and bruises around the victim's wrists and ankles, indicate that she was restrained by cuffs, or manacles at one time...."

As Jim went about his grisly business, he speculated on the circumstances surrounding the woman's demise. The file said she was brought in from Bronson and that the police had a local minister in custody for the crime. Jim wondered what kind of a fiend, especially a man of the cloth, could do such a thing to a pretty young woman like — he consulted the clipboard — Rebecca Langsfelder. Scum like that deserved to be shot down in the street like the mad dogs they were. Similar dark thoughts occupied Jim's mind as he continued this day's unappealing work.

Vint stared through the bars at the wall opposite his cell, not seeing the dingy, institutional green-painted bricks that comprised that wall. He had just returned from a couple of hours of questioning. He couldn't say it was grueling – just boring. The cops would ask the same questions, over and over, until he wanted to scream. His mouth tasted like stale coffee and his skin felt oily and dirty. He would gladly exchange his one phone call for a long, hot shower.

Vint had become pastor of the small Baptist church in Bronson two years ago. The village of Bronson had no more than three hundred and fifty people but Vint was fresh out of seminary and figured it would be a good place to start his ministry. The people were friendly, albeit a bit curious about Vint's big-city manners. The church was well-kept and cheery. The parsonage was as neat as a pin when Vint arrived, and the fridge was stocked with Tupperware containers filled with pre-cooked dishes the ladies on the church welcoming committee had lovingly prepared. Everyone went out of his or her way to be cordial to him. The people were from tough, agricultural stock and worked hard to wrest a living from their rocky farmland. Though unsophisticated, Vint quickly learned they were not stupid, as evidenced by the questions they threw at him after Sunday services.

There were a number of unattached young women in the small congregation and Vint had to admit he had considered them as prospective marriage material. He had grown fond of a couple of them, including Becky, but so far nothing serious had developed, save for a couple of innocuous dates. Now, his whole pastoral life in Bronson was in a shambles. The fact that such a heinous murder could happen in such a quiet, rural community seemed almost inconceivable. As a crowd of faces crossed the screen of Vint's inner eye, he tried to imagine who the culprit could be. No one he knew seemed capable of such a crime. Who would want to kill a sweet girl like Becky Langsfelder—and in such a heinous fashion?

Priscilla Edwina Stephenson pored over the newspaper like her life depended on it. In a way it did, for her chosen occupation depended upon business generated by the events that were chronicled in the newspaper's pages. "Cilla" was a private detective, or at least she hoped to be. Since graduating from the correspondence school she had taken the private detective course from, her job opportunities had been slim. She found a part time gig with a large security firm but the paperwork and chain-of-command of *any* large firm went against her independent grain. She wanted her *own* cases, not the administrivia of some large, by-the-numbers corporation. For now, she depended on the income she derived from the big firm, and some independent insurance surveillance work she did for an established private investigation firm, but she hoped for a breakthrough that would launch her career.

One of the things that militated against her, in her opinion, was the unfortunate combination of names she was saddled with at birth. Why her parents thought Priscilla and Edwina were appropriate names, even for a girl, was beyond her. How could she gain any respect as a private investigator with names like those? In high school, she preferred the nickname Cilla, or sometimes Eddie. Yet, the thought of her ever changing her name wasn't even considered. Her name was just that—her name—and she would rise or fall wearing it. When she had her business cards made, she used the moniker *P. E. Stephenson*.

A small article on page three stopped Cilla's thoughts cold. It mentioned a rape/murder in the village of Bronson, involving a minister named Vinton Montrose, Jr. He was now in custody in the local jail, awaiting arraignment on homicide charges. Though the article was short on details, Cilla got the distinct impression the man was innocent of the charges brought against him. She got out her ballpoint and circled the article, folding the page to keep it prominent.

CHAPTER 2:
STALEMATE

Vint had reached the end of his rope. After two months, the case was no farther along than when he was first arraigned. The police had not been able to bring a case against him after his arraignment due to a lack of incriminating evidence of any kind. They could find no fingerprints at the crime scene. Though it appeared Becky had been raped, there was no semen, or other DNA evidence, to tie him to the crime. It's one thing to arrest and accuse someone, but quite another to make it stick. Vint had been released with the usual admonitions a week after his arrest, but even though the police tossed his apartment and office—vandalism with a warrant in Vint's opinion—they couldn't come up with a shred of proof that he had done the heinous things of which he had been accused. The Chief was almost surly when he slid Vint's personal effects across the desk and he was sent home—with a stern warning not to leave town. Vint suspected the Chief was certain of his guilt and harbored resentment that the law was unable to keep him any longer.

Now, after two months of tense waiting, the police were no farther along on the case. Even the media had relegated the case to yesterday's news. It was still officially open, but there hadn't been a significant break in the case since Vint's arrest. It had come to the point that the department wouldn't even return or pick up his calls to request a status on the case. He was certain they felt they had their man and were waiting for him to eventually trip up.

Vint hated hanging on tenterhooks like this. Every day he would pray to the Lord to be relieved of this burden, that there would be a break in the case and the culprit found. So far the heavens had "become as brass" to his fervent pleas.

Not only was the whole sordid episode a drag on his faith, his church attendance had fallen to nearly nothing. Just the other day there were rumbles of his being evicted from the parsonage the church afforded him as pastor. It was just a matter of time until he was asked to leave. He couldn't blame the townspeople really. They just wanted to put the whole thing behind them and get back to some semblance of normalcy.

Vint now sat in his study, his head in his hands, an open Bible spread before him, and an outline of sermon notes sketchily started. Vint had continued to prepare and preach his Sunday sermons. A few members, in support of their accused pastor, still came to services and Vint felt he owed them his best effort, even though his heart wasn't in it. He didn't know how long he could keep on. The weight of the accusations hung over his head like the Sword of Damocles. Vint began yet another prayer, not knowing an important part of the answer was on its way to him even as he prayed.

At the time Vint was beginning his prayer, Cilla opened the file folder she had kept on the Bronson murder. She had followed the case for a short time, until it had stagnated. She wondered if the young minister was still at his church and how he was holding up. Two months had passed and they, like the case, had been a stagnant time for her too. Cilla had continued to work at her part-time security and insurance jobs, waiting for her ad to be answered, but to no avail. She had yet to get a nibble. She stared at the paltry amount of data on the case before her and had a thought. Perhaps, instead of waiting for business to come her way, she should go out and find it. At about the time Vint was halfway through his prayer, Cilla picked up the telephone and dialed directory assistance.

CHAPTER 3:
INTERVIEW

Vint opened the door to admit the private detective who had called. He was surprised by the diminutive stature of the woman before him. She was indeed short—about five-foot-three—with dark, almost black, shoulder length, straight hair, parted on one side. She had a pleasant, open face, and green eyes. A swath of freckles covered her small nose and plump cheeks, making her look about fifteen years old. Glancing below the neck, however, Vint saw a woman's figure, if a bit full, in contrast to her youthful face. She wore a white, short-sleeved blouse and faded denim skirt. Her small frame seemed to scintillate with suppressed energy. She stuck out her hand.

"Hi! I'm Cilla Stephenson. I know the card I sent you says P. E., but my name's Priscilla Edwina and I couldn't exactly be taken seriously with *those* names, so I...."

"Pleased to meet you Miss Stephenson," Vint said, cutting her off in mid-sentence. He was surprised at the firmness of her handshake, as well as the rapidity of her speech. "I'm Vinton Montrose, Vint to my friends. Shall we go into my office?"

Vint held the door for Cilla to enter and was greeted by a waft of delicate fragrance combined with the fresh air. He gestured down the hall and stepped ahead to lead the way. He stopped by his office door and motioned for Cilla to enter.

"I'm going to leave the door open, if you don't mind," Vint said, going to the chair behind his desk and sitting down, "As a single pastor, I need to observe the proprieties. Please, sit."

Cilla sat, taking in the lanky minister. He seemed like an anachronism, a polite throwback to another era. *Leaving the door open to observe proprieties, indeed!* Cilla thought. She felt like she had stepped back in time. At the same time, Cilla liked what she saw. Vint had a ruggedly handsome face, with none of the pastiness of too much time spent indoors. He also had a lanky, athletic physique. She guessed he spent a lot of time outside the parsonage.

Vint, from his side of the desk, was making observations of his own. In spite of her garrulousness at the door, Cilla Stephenson knew how to keep her peace. He could see she was sizing him up and felt vaguely uneasy at the scrutiny. So, he decided to do some scrutinizing of his own. Upon a second look, Vint noticed that Cilla wasn't as young as she first appeared. She had crow's feet at the corners of her eyes and faint lines around her mouth. Otherwise, her complexion was flawless. She eschewed makeup, kept her eyebrows neat but full and un-penciled, and wore only a medium red lipstick that perfectly complemented her complexion. Her clear-eyed gaze indicated intelligence. Her look and demeanor indicated someone with a high degree of confidence and competence. Vint found himself attracted to her.

"The reason I called you Mr., er, *Reverend* Montrose...."

"Vint. Please call me Vint. Reverend Montrose is far too formal."

"That's the second time you've done that to me, *Reverend Montrose*. Are you in the habit of stepping on people's introductions?"

Cilla's directness surprised Vint. "Oh, I... I'm sorry Miss Stephenson. I apologize for my rudeness. I assure you it was unintentional."

Cilla's anger subsided at Vint's humble manner. He certainly seemed to lack an overlarge ego. "That's okay. I have a tendency to come on too strong sometimes. To get to my point, I called you two weeks ago because your case seems to have dead-ended and I thought I could help. You see, as a private investigator devoted solely to your case, I feel I could possibly get things moving again."

"I see," Vint said simply, "So you have experience in these types of things?" He could see Cilla's face color to the roots of her dark hair.

It was Cilla's turn to be nonplused. "I…uh… well I…no," Cilla said, her confidence deflating a little. "No, I have no field experience with this kind of thing. You see, I just got my certificate and, aside from some part-time security and insurance work, I haven't had a case. I don't know why either. I *aced* my courses and have *real instincts* for the job. I know I'll be a great private investigator if only…." With that, Cilla ran out of gas.

Vint had to work at not smiling. It wouldn't do to insult the woman at this point. His heart went out to her, she looked so small and fragile at that moment. His attraction to her grew even more. "I tell you what, Cilla. Why don't we go to lunch? Maggie's Diner down the street makes a great meatloaf on Tuesdays. We could order some and discuss your approach to your first case."

"*Really?*" Cilla blurted out, "I *love* meatloaf!" Then she straightened. "That would be nice. I'm a bit hungry at that."

"…So, I think the local police have given up on the case." Cilla said around a mouthful of meatloaf. "Not that they don't *want* to catch the girl's killer—they just think they already have their man."

"That's exactly how I feel," Vint said, thoughtfully chewing his meal, "like they're just waiting for me to slip up."

"Uh-huh. Now, what I propose to do is start at the beginning, ask to see the evidence the police have, and extensively question the folks around here. Despite what the TV shows say, ninety-five percent of detective work is in the details. You *have* to do your homework."

"There's just one small detail," Vint brought up.

"What's that?"

"I'm sorry if I misled you before, indicating that I would hire you. It's your fee. I'm just a poor preacher. Having just started, my savings are minuscule. I can't afford a private investigator's fee, even one who's just starting out."

Cilla put down her fork and lowered her hands to the table. She finished chewing her mouthful and swallowed. "You know why it is I like meatloaf — especially diner meatloaf?" Vint shook his head. "Because it's a good way to find out what kind of food they serve. If the meatloaf's good, then it's a fairly sure bet the rest of the food will be prepared well. I like diner food. It's honest — no pretense — just good, solid food to fill up an empty stomach." Cilla stopped and looked seriously at Vint. "As corny as it seems, I tend to look at clients that way. Just seeing the sign out front is one thing — it's the quality of the food on the menu, so to speak, that impresses me."

"So, do I measure up as a 'good meatloaf' kind of guy?" Vint asked, smiling.

"Oh...I'm not trying to compare you to

meatloaf…you're more like fillet mign…" Cilla began, hesitating and blushing again.

"I'm just kidding with you," Vint said, trying to let Cilla off the hook, "I get your point; there's no need to be embarrassed."

Cilla looked at Vint and blinked. "Anyway, I was going to insist on a fee, so you wouldn't think I was desperate but, the truth is, I *am* desperate. Look, I won't try to kid you. I'll agree to do the case gratis. If I crack it, the publicity would make me a somebody in this business. All it requires is for you to have enough faith in my abilities to take me on. What do you say?"

Vint sat back in the booth. "Okay, I'll agree to your terms on two conditions."

"And what would they be?" Cilla said with a suspicious look on her face.

"One…that I pay you *something*."

"That would be okay," Cilla said, smiling, "What's the other?"

"That I work with you."

Cilla's smile vanished.

When they had eaten lunch, they returned to Vint's office and Cilla conducted some preliminary questioning.

"So let's begin with Becky Langsfelder," Cilla said without preamble, taking out a small, digital recorder. "Mind if I record this?" Vint shook his head. "I like to record interviews to get a feel for the emotions and nuances behind the person's comments. It can tell me more than the actual words. So, how well did you know Becky?"

"She was a parishioner in my congregation," Vint answered.

"*Just* a parishioner?" Cilla asked, noting how Vint's lips compressed as if biting back a retort.

"Oh goody — another round of probing questions," Vint complained, "As if the police weren't enough."

Cilla was impressed at Vint's self-control. He certainly seemed to live up to his role as preacher. "I'm not going to grill you, if that's what you're worried about, but I *do* need to get some of the salient facts directly from you."

"Sorry — didn't mean to whine. Becky is...*was* a very attractive woman and I *am* single after all. We dated some but I didn't see the relationship going anywhere." Vint paused to sigh. "To be frank, Becky impressed me as entirely too eager for a husband."

Again Cilla saw no evidence of anything simmering beneath the surface. Vint's answers were straightforward and without rancor. "I see. Tell me, are there any personality traits you have — say, a hot temper — that would make the police suspect you?"

Vint smiled. "No, I'm a pretty regular guy in my dealings with others — pretty mundane in my habits and actions — kind of boring really."

Cilla looked at the man in front of her and thought he was anything *but* boring. "Is that how you think of yourself — as boring?"

"Look." Vint said with an exasperated sigh. He was impressed by Cilla's simple-but-probing questions but not in the mood to be grilled after all he had gone through with the police. "I consider myself a fairly normal guy. I'm regular in my habits and I'm not given to flamboyant behavior. Some people might consider that boring — okay? Perhaps it's why I chose to be a minister."

"Fine. Can you tell me where you were the night Rebecca Langsfelder was murdered?"

Again with the probing, Vint thought, but his admiration for this intense young woman cut her some slack and elicited an answer. "I was right here in my study, preparing for the mid-week prayer meeting. I don't have an alibi for the exact time she was killed, but I was down to Maggie's for supper about an hour before. Kathy — she's a waitress there — already told the police she had served me supper."

"Okay then." Cilla concluded. "I'm going to be poking around town for the next few days — see what I can scare up. Thanks for your patience." She switched off the recorder and looked up at Vint.

"Fine," Vint responded, wondering if Cilla's no-nonsense manner was compensation for her trying to make it in a typically male profession, "Supper?"

"Excuse me?" Cilla asked, caught off guard by the matter-of-fact offer.

"Would you like to join me again for supper? You're new in town and I could use the company. It wouldn't be a breach of protocol would it?"

"I'm having trouble getting a reading on you," Cilla said without a smile.

"What do you mean by that?" Vint said, clearly surprised, "Am I that mysterious?"

"Well, you answer my questions readily enough. That's one thing. But I get the impression you don't think a woman should be doing what I'm doing."

Vint was now becoming annoyed. "Look Miss...Cilla. You were the one who waltzed in here bold as brass and insisted I take you on. You admitted yourself that you're fresh out of school. Pardon my being blunt but I don't know enough *about* you to form any kind of opinion."

Cilla seemed to deflate, her aggressive, go-get-'em manner replaced by a look of defeat. Vint's annoyance was dissipated by her dejection. He drew in a deep breath and let it out.

"Cilla, we seem to be getting off on the wrong foot here. Believe me, outside of a bit of bantering, and the fact I think you're somewhat inexperienced, I have no personal animus toward you. I'm afraid you seem to have the ability to get under my skin for reasons I find hard to describe. You're much more direct than any of the women I've known. I suppose it puts me off a little. Can't we call a truce and have a nice dinner together?"

Cilla's spirits seemed to rise a bit. "I suppose you're right about the 'direct' part. I do tend to come on strong. I'll try to be a little more tactful. Supper would be fine. It must be the country air or something but I'm starved already and I just had lunch a few hours ago! I'm also bushed from the trip. I'm going to try and catch a quick nap. I'm at what appears to be the only accommodations in town — Anna's boarding house. Just knock on my door when it's time to go. I'm in room three."

Vint looked across the table at his supper companion. They had gone to Vinny Russotto's little restaurant. It was a classic, family-owned Italian place with red-checked tablecloths, dim, romantic lighting, and Chianti bottles with candles in them. Their candle was lit and its light flickered on Cilla's round face. Her glossy black hair framed her face, and the candlelight minimized her freckles — making her look older. Vint thought she looked very appealing.

"This is good food!" Cilla exclaimed, putting down her glass of Chianti, "I haven't tasted any better anywhere in the city."

"Yeah, these small town places can surprise you. But you still can't get a decent bagel to save your life," Vint said, chuckling.

"Or try to find a good pizza in New England, outside of Boston," Cilla added.

"When is a good pizza not a pizza?"

"Pardon?" Cilla said around another mouthful

of pasta.

"I know of a place where you can get the best pizza, but they don't call it by that name there."

"Ooo, ooo...I know that!" Cilla said, holding up her hand and reaching for the wineglass with the other. She took a drink to clear her mouth. "Let me think—Trenton, New Jersey!"

"Give the little lady a pick off the top row. And do you know what they *do* call them?"

"Tomato pies."

"That answer scores a bonus prize, little lady," Vint said in his best John Wayne imitation.

Cilla laughed. "Y'know, you're not at all the boring guy you claim to be. You're quite funny actually."

"Well!" Vint did his Jack Benny impression this time. "Take a girl to dinner and she calls you *funny*."

Cilla laughed even harder, so hard that she snorted, which made her break up all the more. Vint liked this side of her. She was a vivacious woman, full of energy and enthusiasm. In spite of their earlier friction, he found himself attracted to her more and more.

"So, what made you want to become a private eye?"

"That's private *investigator*, mister," Cilla said, with a twinkle in her eye, "Actually, I like the independence of the job—a far cry from my nine-to-five as a bank teller."

"You were a bank teller? I can't imagine a

person with your verve sitting behind a counter. It must have driven you crazy."

"Tell me about it! That's why I took the correspondence course in my spare time. I haven't had much luck with cases though. I know I'm good at the details and I have patience to boot. I'll be a great investigator someday."

"*Correspondence* course?" Vint blurted out, feeling like he stepped on a land mine, "You got your diploma through the *mail*?"

"You bet!" Cilla said, refusing to take offense at the implication, "In some ways, it's a lot harder than a classroom environment. You're completely on your own. The advantage is, you can take your time over the more difficult subjects — work at your own pace. Nevertheless, I got through it months early."

"Please don't take offense, but perhaps that's why you're finding cases hard to come by."

"What — you think I put it in my ads — *correspondence school trained private investigator, seeking employment*? No, it's just hard to break into the business. You have to establish a track record."

"Did you ever think of working for an established private detective firm?"

Cilla became defensive. "I do security and insurance work on the side," she said, annoyed at her new client's continued implications. She didn't like having to audition for someone obviously ignorant of what a private investigator did.

"You didn't answer my question."

Cilla studied Vint's face for so long, he didn't think she'd answer. In fact, she almost didn't. "I worked for a guy once. But, aside from the fact he failed to take me seriously — like you — he had a problem keeping his hands to himself. I had to persuade him to stop by sticking my revolver in his stomach. That was the end of that job. Does that answer your question fully?"

"I'm sorry to hear that," Vint said, realizing he had insulted Cilla, "Is there a man in your life?" he asked, changing the subject.

Cilla's eyebrows shot up. This constant change of tack was becoming disorienting.

"Hey, I'm a pastor after all," Vint said, smiling, "It comes with the territory. You're supposed to confide in me at this point."

"Professionally speaking?"

"Of course," Vint answered, still smiling, "Just as detecting is your area of expertise, pastoring's mine."

"Is that a real word — *pastoring*?"

"Come to think of it, it probably isn't but it does convey the idea, doesn't it?"

"Probably as good as *detecting*. No, I don't have anyone I'm with — just a couple of dates, none of them as much fun as this one." Realizing her blunder, Cilla looked up, her face coloring yet again. She realized she was doing that a lot around this man. He was really getting to her.

She opened her mouth to correct herself.

Vint held up a hand to stop her explanation. "I know what you meant and I'm flattered. But I guess it *is* a dinner date after all, when you get right down to it. What say we continue to pretend it's a date and take a walk? It's a beautiful evening and it *is* the country after all — very romantic."

"In that case, it's a good thing you're a minister," Cilla said in mock seriousness and they both laughed.

A small river ran by Bronson, close to Main Street. Vint and Cilla walked along an asphalt path next to the water. A couple of bicyclists and joggers passed them in both directions every once in awhile. The evening was indeed beautiful and the moist earth and greenery smelled wonderful. It was truly a romantic setting.

The two of them walked in silence, occasionally looking at one another and smiling.

In spite of her energy, she knows how to keep her own counsel, Vint thought. "It's funny," he said, breaking the silence.

"What is?"

"Well, you're here because I've been accused of murder. Yet, you accepted both my lunch and supper invitations. Now we're walking together, alone by the river. I thought nothing of it because I *know* I didn't do it, but you aren't privy to my thoughts. Aren't you at least a *little* afraid to be alone with me?"

Cilla stopped. Vint took a couple of steps, realized he had left her behind, and turned to face her.

"If I thought for a moment that you murdered Becky Langsfelder, I wouldn't have even taken the case," Cilla said softly, "I was convinced of your innocence without having met you and now that I have, I'm even more convinced."

Looking at the man in front of her, Cilla felt a wave of affection wash over her. It came — unexpected and unbidden — yet there it was. She didn't normally let her emotions rule her. By rights, she should be more cautious. After all, Ted Bundy was a charmer, who disarmed women with his affable manner and good looks. Yet, somehow, Cilla felt safe with this man. She seemed to know instinctively that she had nothing to fear from him — that fate had cruelly singled him out for grief.

She started walking again and Vint fell in alongside her. They hadn't gone too far when she reached out and took Vint's hand.

Vint looked over at her and she smiled up at him. "Thanks for believing in me," he said, "And thanks for *this*." He lifted the hand with Cilla's in it.

Vint's innocuous comments set off Cilla's emotional brakes — things were moving too fast. "Well, you were right — it *is* romantic. I didn't want to spoil the mood. After all we *are* pretending this is a date, right?"

Vint smiled and squeezed Cilla's small hand. She squeezed back. They walked slowly down the river path, each savoring the beautiful evening, each thinking private thoughts.

Chapter 4:
Confessions

Among the first things Cilla did for Vint was to go to the Bronson police and ask for as much evidence on the case as she could get. She drove down to headquarters — located in a small, brick building that could have been an animal hospital at one time — and asked to see the chief of police. Cilla studied the place from her seat in front of the police desk. It was a tiny department, but well ordered. There appeared to be only one office — the Chief's — and four desks in the main area. One of them, nearest the office, was occupied by a well-dressed, professional-looking, woman secretary — also probably the Chief's. A man in a cheap suit — probably a detective, occupied one of the other two. The third desk belonged to an attractive blonde woman in a police uniform. She was on the telephone. The forth was not occupied at present. Another patrol officer? After a half-hour wait — one she was convinced was to show her who was in control — the secretary answered her phone, returned the receiver to its cradle, and got up to walk to where Cilla was sitting.

"Chief Kroeger will see you, Miss Stephenson," she said in a pleasant contralto voice and ushered her into the Chief's office.

"Hello, Chief Kroeger," Cilla said, smiling and extending her hand.

Kroeger shook it briskly, not bothering to rise from his seat. "Have a seat. What can I do for you?"

So much for the proprieties, Cilla thought as she sat down, *Might as well just dive in.* "I'm a private investigator, working for Reverend Montrose," Cilla said, sliding a leather holder containing her private investigator's identification toward the chief, "and I'm here to ask you for some information on the Langsfelder case."

Kroeger picked up the ID and his face took on a frown. "I assume you're aware that Reverend Montrose is a suspect in what is an open case."

"Yes sir, I'm aware of that. But, things seem to have come to a standstill—largely because you have no evidence against him—and I was hoping to be able to help one way or the other."

"Are you trying to say that the police aren't up to doing their job?" the chief said, frowning as he slid Cilla's ID back toward her.

"Oh, no sir. I'm just here to offer whatever help I can."

"This is an open case, Miss Stephenson. And I'm not sure we need your...."

"Please, sir—all I'm asking is that you let me

see the evidence. You can redact any names of other suspects you wish. I just want to see what you've found, so I can make some hypotheses. Is that asking too much?" Cilla hoped her smile and friendly tone would win the day.

The chief pondered her request for a few seconds. "I want you to understand that it is not the policy of this department to allow this, but I see no harm in letting you see some of the evidence. However, if you push too hard, or make a nuisance of yourself, I'll shut you down. Understood?"

"Oh, yes sir! I won't be a problem at all. Thank you for your help."

The chief pressed a button on his intercom. "Alma, send Susie in."

"Yes sir," a metallic female voice answered.

Cilla sat uncomfortably while they waited. Then she noticed a framed photo of a young woman on the credenza next to the window. It appeared to be a high school graduation photo. It was of the blonde officer she saw at one of the desks outside.

"Is that your daughter Chief?"

The chief looked over at the picture and smiled. "Sure is. She's a ringer for her mother. Pretty girl — good she doesn't take after me."

"She's a very pretty girl all right. But don't sell yourself short. She looks a lot like you. In fact, I've noted that attractive women usually look a lot like their fathers in most cases."

"Really?" the chief said, his eyebrows going up.

At that second, Susie entered the office.

"Miss Stephenson, this is Officer Susan Kroeger."

Cilla stood and shook hands with the woman. "Hi—pleased to meet you. Please, call me Cilla."

"Hello Cilla. I understand you're looking for information on the Langsfelder case?"

"Uh-huh."

"Susie, take her to talk with Don," the Chief said. "You'll be her liaison. Let Don be the judge of what Miss Stephenson should see. Okay?"

"Yes sir. Miss St...*Cilla*, come with me. We'll go see detective Franzer. He's at Maggie's diner, having lunch. He's the primary investigator on the case. We can walk—it's close."

On the way over to see Franzer, Susie asked Cilla a question. "So, what made you decide to be a private detective?"

"Please don't take this the wrong way, but what made you decide to be a police officer?"

"You mean, aside from the fact Dad's the Chief?"

Both women chuckled. Cilla was the first to speak. "I've always been fascinated with criminalistics. I also like working for myself."

"What about joining the police force?"

"Are you kidding? I don't exactly make the height requirement. Look at you. What are you—five-ten?"

"I see your point. Five-eleven, actually. Like you, I find police work fascinating. I had to fight like hell to get more than a desk job—protective dad, and all that."

"Good for you. Go for it, I say."

Susan introduced Cilla to Franzer when they got to the diner and they joined him for lunch. Franzer was a slender, intense, dark-haired man who wore a rumpled, but expensive suit. He seemed to be one of those men who had a perpetual five-o'clock shadow. But, he was affable enough and didn't seem to bristle at being asked to provide Cilla with some information on the Langsfelder case. They chatted through lunch and went back to the station. Franzer had Alma copy much of the file and give it to Cilla in a fresh folder after he had blacked out some lines. He also had her copy the crime scene photos. Cilla thanked Susan and him profusely, said her good-byes, and left.

Cilla pored over the file in her van after she left the station. She had about as much info as she was going to get for the moment. She had seemed to hit it off with Susie *and* Detective Franzer, however, and figured she would have their continued cooperation during the ongoing investigation. After reading, what became immediately evident to Cilla was the fact that they thought Vint was the culprit and had somehow managed to hide his culpability from everyone. Her initial hunch having been proved correct, she was determined to prove them wrong.

Cilla decided to visit the Langsfelders and question them. She hoped they'd agree and not become hostile. She was still hoping when she rang their front bell. An older version of Becky opened the door, a pleasant smile on her face. The usual Jehovah's Witnesses and other solicitors obviously didn't visit the residents of Bronson.

"May I help you?" Mrs. Langsfelder asked.

"Hi, I'm Cilla Stephenson," Cilla said, extending her hand, which held her business card.

Mrs. Langsfelder looked at it and back to Cilla. "A private investigator? I don't understand."

"I'm assisting the police in the investigation into your daughter's...." Cilla answered, leaving the obvious unsaid.

"The police called you in?"

"No, not exactly."

"Then...someone hired you?"

"Yes, I work for Reverend Montrose."

Mrs. Langsfelder's pleasant demeanor hardened. "You work for the man accused of killing my daughter? What makes you think I'll talk to you?"

"You and your husband, actually. I won't lie to you, Mrs. Langsfelder. I represent Reverend Montrose because I believe he's innocent, and I want to clear his name. But more than that, I want to bring the real culprit to justice."

Five minutes later, Cilla was sitting in the Langsfelder's living room with a cup of tea, and her recorder, in front of her.

"I'll try to be as sensitive to your loss as I possibly can," Cilla said to the couple opposite her, "but please understand if I ask a question that brings up a painful memory." Mr. and Mrs. Langsfelder nodded solemnly. "Could you tell me who else Becky dated before she dated Reverend Montrose?"

"Becky was a serious girl," Mrs. Langsfelder began, "always studying hard up in her room, so she didn't see many boys. Oh, she went on picnics and swimming outings with the young people from church and school — that sort of thing...."

"She had a steady boyfriend in her senior year of high school," Mr. Langsfelder added, "His name was Bobby Miller. He was a year ahead of Becky. When he went off to college, they seemed to have lost touch. Becky was sad about that for awhile — didn't date for a long time."

"Oh yes," Mrs. Langsfelder remembered, "Becky went out with that young man from Altoona — Tommy Neulander — from time to time. He was a nice boy. I told Becky she should think more seriously about him."

"How did she react to that?" Cilla asked.

"She told me she liked Tommy but he didn't "click" with her. I wondered what it was she was looking for."

"Oh? Why did you think that?" Cilla

asked, "Did she seem to have impossibly high standards?"

"Not high enough," Mr. Langsfelder interjected.

"Why do you say that, sir?'

"She dated that bum Stuart Loeb pretty heavily for awhile. Never liked the kid. Too much of a smart aleck. He was respectful of us and all, but I always thought he was too oily, too cocksure of himself — like he was God's gift."

"Oh, Kurt," Mrs. Langsfelder chided, "You were always scaring off suitors. No one was ever good enough for your Becky."

Kurt looked at his wife and gave her a look of pure sadness. "I wish I would have been even more critical of her dating, Celia. Maybe we would still have her with us."

Celia, realizing her inadvertent blunder, teared up and began sniffling. She dropped her head, pulled a tissue from her apron pocket, and began dabbing at her eyes.

"Would you like to take a break?" Cilla asked. Celia shook her head and Kurt remained silent, so Cilla continued. "Did Becky break it off with Loeb when she started dating Reverend Montrose?"

"Yes," Kurt answered, "and I was glad for it. Vint—Reverend Montrose—is a great guy. Liked him the minute I saw him — solid citizen — no beating around the bush. I can't understand to this day why on earth Becky broke it off with him. They seemed so good together."

"Did Becky see anyone else after that?"

"Not that I ever noticed. She was pretty broken up about Vint," Kurt answered.

"Well, thank you for you time," Cilla concluded, "And I'm sorry to bring up so many painful memories. But you were a great help."

"You really think so?" Celia asked, sniffling.

"Yes indeed," Cilla reassured her, "Sometimes the smallest detail can make the difference. May I come back and ask some more questions as they occur to me?"

"Sure, if it will help catch the monster that killed our Becky," Kurt said, "But you be careful too. You're just a slip of a girl yourself."

"I certainly will," Cilla assured him, pleased at his "slip of a girl" comment.

A couple of days later, Vint asked Cilla a question. "Would you like to come to the service on Sunday? With my connections, I can get you a good seat."

Cilla really didn't want to go but thought it would be rude to decline. "Sure. When's the service?"

"During the spring and summer, the services start at 10 AM. I'll stop by the boarding house."

"Okay, thanks."

Cilla was appalled at how empty the church was. Including her, there were only six in the congregation. She noticed Kurt and Celia among them. *Loyal to the end*, she thought. Vint hadn't been kidding when he said the accusations had an effect on church attendance. But, to his credit, he didn't slack off on his sermon. He proved to be an able preacher — not the pulpit pounding kind, but animated and engaging. Cilla found herself listening intently. What impressed her was the fact that — aside from it being a sermon — there was little "religiosity." Vint spoke of God as though he were a personal friend. She wondered if it could really be that way. She remembered some preacher from her past saying that God was like a father. Well, if that were true, she could do without knowing God *that* well.

Walking on their way to lunch after the service, this time at one of the parishioner's houses, Vint and Cilla talked.

"So, what did you think?" Vint asked, wondering what kind of faith Cilla had.

"I liked your sermon very much," Cilla said casually.

"Well, that's a relief. I thought the absence of a congregation would put you off a bit," Vint said, disappointed. Cilla's bland answer gave him no further clues as to Cilla's faith.

"Look, I understand why there are so few people. But, it wasn't the fault of your preaching. You speak about God as if you know him personally."

Ah, a clue, Vint thought. "Yes — I do. I don't think of my faith as a religion. It's more of a relationship."

"Don't tell me—God speaks to you?" Cilla shot back, her eyebrows raised into question marks.

Vint looked at Cilla and smiled. "Oh, I get it. You want to know if I hear a voice from above, telling me what to do."

"Do you?" Cilla asked, worried.

"I don't hear an audible voice coming from heaven. But, I feel he speaks to me from out of his word, the Bible, and when he answers my prayers."

"He answers your prayers?" Cilla asked, relieved that Vint wasn't some Jesus freak. Nevertheless, his answer intrigued her.

"Certainly." Vint could see Cilla was genuinely interested to know what he would say. He prayed inwardly that he wouldn't botch it. "A wise man once said that God *always* answers prayer. Sometimes the answer is yes, sometimes it's no, and sometimes it's wait awhile."

"Hmmm—interesting viewpoint. But you have a better track record than me, I guess. God and I aren't exactly on speaking terms."

"When was the last time you spoke with him—prayed, I mean?"

"Ouch," Cilla said, uncomfortable at how close Vint was coming with his questions.

"My question wasn't meant as a dig. It's my guess you're pretty much convinced that God wouldn't be at all interested in little old you. Too unimportant to concern him — is that it?"

"No, that's not it at all," Cilla said, parrying Vint's question because of how close he was to the truth, "I just never thought of God in that way. He always seemed so stern on those infrequent times I went to church."

"What — you *saw* him at your church?" Vint said, smiling to defuse the jibe.

"No. Stop trying to be funny. The priest just portrayed him that way."

"Catholic?"

"Yeah."

"Well, some people tend to approach God a lot more seriously than most."

"Wow, I'm impressed," Cilla said. She *was* impressed — by Vint's gentle way of getting to the core of things. "You could have taken a serious shot, but you didn't."

"Just because I'm an evangelical Protestant, doesn't mean I have an ax to grind with the Pope. It's just that I don't think God's some stern old man, waiting to push the misery button when you or I seem to be having too much fun." Vint was heartened by Cilla's honesty — and the fact she was opening up to him regarding her faith.

"Pardon my saying it, but you don't seem to be having much fun of late," Cilla observed.

Vint's elation turned to disappointment. He looked into Cilla's eyes. "You have a point there. But, it's not God's fault. Plus, my problems are temporary. Poor Becky's the one who's dead."

Cilla noticed that she had scored a hit on Vint's impregnable religious armor. "See? That's what I mean. Why'd a nice kid like her get killed in such a horrible way? Where was God then?"

"Where he always is — watching over us," Vint offered, praying for guidance.

"Isn't that a cop-out?"

"How so?"

"Well, with that kind of 'watching over,' I won't be looking him up as a baby-sitter, thank you very much."

"Whoa — I detect some anger there," Vint said, stinging at the barb in Cilla's comment, "Was there something in your past that caused it?"

Cilla smiled a wry smile. "Very good, pastor. You have the moves, all right. But look, I've had a nice time so far today. Do you think we could forgo all the God-talk and just enjoy it?"

"Sure, if that's what you want," Vint answered, hoping his answer sounded non-committal. He feared he had tried to get too close, too soon.

"Yes, it is," Cilla said, regretting the harshness of her words even as she spoke them.

A couple of days after Cilla had begun to work for Vint, another young woman was murdered in a suburb of Altoona. Though the circumstances of the crime were quite similar, the Altoona police weren't attributing it to the Bronson murderer. The last thing they wanted was to give rise to stories of a serial killer. Realizing it would just be a matter of time before the Bronson police brought Vint in for questioning, Cilla took the initiative and went to Altoona to interview the coroner.

"Thank you for seeing me, Mr. Fournier," Cilla said, sticking out her hand.

"Perhaps you might want to forgo the formalities for the moment," Fournier said, holding up a gloved hand, "I just came from my work."

"Uh, okay. Would you by any chance be working on the latest murder victim?"

"Yes," Fournier said, his expression growing stern.

"Do you think it would be possible for me to have a look? I'm investigating this case in connection with another murder that occurred two months ago."

"The Langsfelder murder?"

"Yes! Boy, you sure have a good memory."

"I don't get so many bodies through here that I would forget the murder of a pretty young woman that easily."

"Would it be okay for me to observe you at work? I'd consider it good training for my chosen profession."

"I don't quite get the connection. You're a private detective, right?"

"Yes, but I try to learn as much as I can."

"Well, it's not really policy to let...."

"Please?" Cilla asked, trying out her best pleading look.

"And then there's the squeamishness thing...."

"Don't worry about me. I have a cast-iron stomach—a regular tomboy growing up."

Fournier looked at Cilla's plump form, wondered about the validity of the tomboy assertions, but relented. "Okay, but you can't interfere in any way. I'll get you a lab coat—and a barf bag. Follow me."

Cilla saw the young woman's body lying nude on the table. A pang hit her heart when she saw how young she was.

"Are you going to be okay?" Fournier asked, looking askance at her.

"Yeah, I...well, she's naked...and she looks so young."

"We'd find it hard to do our work if they had clothes on. And, yes, she's young—too young for this place."

"What's her name?"

Fournier looked down at his fact sheet. "Stiglitz...Amanda Stiglitz."

"How old is she?"

"Eighteen."

Cilla felt another pang at the announcement of her age.

"Okay, I'm going to get started," Fournier said trying to move Cilla past her empathy, "Please don't get in my way. And, *please*, don't talk or ask questions—I'll be recording."

Cilla watched as Fournier went about the grisly task of examining Amanda Stiglitz's corpse, speaking into a microphone about what he found. She appeared to be Cilla's height but not nearly as heavy. In fact, she appeared to be gaunt. Anorexia? Her hip and shoulder bones jutted out, looking like they might pierce her pale, white skin. Multiple contusions and bruises, all over her body, seemed consistent with the facts of Becky Langsfelder's murder. Cilla was so fascinated with the examination, she didn't feel the slightest nausea, even when Fournier got to the Y incision. Before she knew it, Fournier was finished.

"Thank you *so much* for letting me observe," Cilla said appreciatively, after Fournier had finished.

"No problem. You did well—not a hint of nausea."

"I guess I was so fascinated, I forgot about my stomach."

"It was a nice change of pace to have a lay person as an observer. It's usually an evaluator, checking up on my thoroughness."

"You said she appears to have been raped but there was no sign of semen—just like the Langsfelder case. And, you also said she appears to have been naked for a long time. That was also a factor in Becky's case as well. Do you think the two murders might have been committed by the same person?"

"The police say it's not the work of a serial killer," Fournier answered.

"I know what *they* said. What do *you* say?"

"I'd say it was the same person. But, you didn't hear that from me."

"Thank you, Mr. Fournier."

"Jim," Fournier said, smiling, "After all, you've been looking over my shoulder for almost an hour."

"Okay — Jim. Thank you again."

Fournier took Cilla's extended hand. "You're working for the accused pastor in Bronson?"

"Yeah. Why?"

"Aren't the police still on the case?"

"Mr....Jim, I'm afraid the police don't always work as efficiently as you do. They think they have their man in Vint Montrose, so they're, shall we say, not pursuing the case as diligently as they could."

"So you think this Montrose fellow is innocent?"

"As a matter of fact, I do. He's a young minister, fresh out of seminary, and this has devastated him. His life's in the toilet and I'm going to find out who the culprit is before someone flushes it."

Vint and Cilla sat in the large swing on the porch of the parsonage. It was one of those spectacular summer nights that only the country provided. The stars were huge and numerous and seemed ripe for the plucking. The three-quarter moon hung brightly in the eastern sky.

"You sure can't see skies like this in Philadelphia," Cilla observed.

"That's for sure," Vint agreed. He looked over at Cilla, on the other side of the swing, as far away from him as she could get. Sitting there, looking up at the moon, her flawless complexion milky in the moonlight, Vint could see a loveliness that wasn't as evident in the daylight. It was a classic, romantic moment. Right about now, as in the movies he had seen, the violins would start, she would look at him and in seconds be in his arms. Vint couldn't say he would object to the idea.

At that second, Cilla looked at him, "Y'know, I've been thinking about what you told me earlier."

"About the case?"

"No, about — well, about God and all."

"Sounds like it's hard for you to mention God's name."

Cilla's eyes glinted like gems in the pale light. "Yeah, well he and I haven't been on the best of terms."

"Want to talk about it?"

Cilla looked at Vint. Then she dropped her gaze. "I was raised by alcoholics. From the time I was old enough, I took care of them when I wasn't in school. I'd come home to find the house a mess, my mom passed out on the sofa. So, I'd clean up and cook supper. Dad would stagger in later, drunk from visiting the bar he stopped in on the way home. He was more reliable than my mother and managed to keep his job at the plant. But he made up for it on the weekends."

"That's a tough row to hoe for a kid growing up."

"Tell me about it — not that it cut into my social life in school. I may look plump to you now, but I was a regular five-by-five pudgette in school. Boys never gave me a second look."

"You've had a tough life. I can see that. But what got you and God on bad terms? You seem so bitter about it. Did you feel God was being unfair?"

Cilla merely looked at Vint. "It wasn't a matter of fair. I just learned to fend for myself. I never asked for his help — not that I saw much of it — didn't think I needed it anyway."

"It's a pity, too. He would have listened. But how can you be so sure he didn't help you?"

"It doesn't look like he's done much to help you — you being a minister and all." Cilla regretted the cut even as she said it.

Vint's anger flared over her cutting remark but he could see Cilla regretted saying it. She must have noticed his agitation, for she softened a bit.

"I'm sorry. You didn't deserve that. It's just that God doesn't seem to be in the business of looking after his own — know what I mean? Look at all the evil in the world."

Vint looked over at Cilla. Their eyes met. "I find it interesting how quick people are to blame God for all the world's problems. It doesn't seem to work the other way though — he gets no credit for the good. Look, God isn't some cosmic baby-sitter. He doesn't look for skinned knees to stick Band-Aids on. He wants us to be like his Son — whatever happens."

"What do you mean?"

"Well, if God just wanted to fix the world's problems, Jesus wouldn't have had to come to be crucified on a cross."

"Now you're losing me. Isn't that *exactly* what he came to do? At least that's what they used to tell me in Sunday School."

"You went to Sunday School?" Vint asked, smiling.

"Yeah...why? What's so funny about that?"

"Your *parents* sent you to Sunday School?"

"Yes. My mother was adamant about it. She even came to the annual Christmas plays I was in."

Vint chuckled, further irritating Cilla. "Don't you see? God was working in your life even when you had no use for him. And he worked *through your parents*."

"Okay, so suppose I go along with that. What about Jesus dying?"

Vint knew he had to choose his words carefully

at this point. "When Jesus was on this earth, he healed the sick and performed other miracles. But it wasn't because he was some cosmic do-gooder. That wasn't why he came to earth. Those miracles were a confirmation that he was the Messiah, the Savior. Neither God nor Jesus promises us a smooth ride through this life. What's important is that we're written in his Book of Life. It doesn't matter what befalls us here, as long as we know we can go to be with him when this life is over."

"But that all sounds so simplistic, so 'pie-in-the-sky.'"

"In a way it does, but this life isn't all there is. It's just the beginning. Haven't you ever sensed that?"

Cilla dropped her head. Vint could see she was struggling with the principles he had just shown her. She was such an independent, self-sufficient little thing. First, she had to overcome that to trust what he was telling her. Then, she had to trust a God she could not see, and trust him enough to put her life in his hands. Vint prayed silently that the Holy Spirit would guide her to faith. Silence lay between them like some stern chaperone.

Cilla could feel Vint's eyes on her as surely as though he had laid his hand on her shoulder. This man had affected her like no other in her short life. She was attracted to him, but his earnest, simplistic faith made her want to push him away. The last thing she wanted from him was a sermon. She wanted him to put his arms around her and kiss her passionately — to let her vent some of her pent-up attraction. Yet, even as she thought this, she was embarrassed by her feelings. She felt they were unworthy of such a good man — that they would sully something pure and holy.

Vint had resigned himself to just sitting with Cilla in silence, when she did something that surprised him. She reached out and took his hand. There were no sexual overtones to it — she just interlaced her fingers with his and clasped his hand tightly. Then she slid over next to him and gently rested her head on his shoulder. In a few seconds, Vint could feel her body shake as she began to cry. Vint put his arm around Cilla's shoulders. He anticipated that she would stiffen and withdraw but, instead, she turned into his chest and poured out her emotions in hot tears Vint could feel through his shirt. He didn't say a word but put his other arm around her small shoulders and rocked with her as she cried. A welter of thoughts swirled in his brain as he sat there and smelled her tears, mingled with the delicate, floral fragrance that emanated from her dark hair.

After a long while, Cilla sniffled and sat up, fishing in her purse for a Kleenex. The front of Vint's shirt was soaked with her tears. They felt as pure as holy water to him.

"I'm sor...." Cilla began to say but Vint

stopped her by taking her chin in his left hand, plucking the limp tissue from hers and daubing at her eyes.

"You have nothing to apologize for. If I can't recognize genuine emotion, then I'm definitely in the wrong vocation. No explanation is needed."

Cilla sniffled again. She reached up and touched Vint's wet shirt. "I've made a mess of your shirt," she said in a small voice.

"It'll dry."

Cilla raised her eyes to look at Vint. "You're not at all what I expected."

"Nor are you," Vint answered. He leaned down and placed a gentle kiss on Cilla's forehead.

Cilla leaned against Vint's chest again and they sat there in the porch swing for a long time, listening to the night-symphony of the Pennsylvania country evening. The Mormon Tabernacle Choir could not have sounded better.

A couple of days later, Cilla stopped by the parsonage around 9AM.

"Good morning," Vint said, "What's up?"

"I've got some business to attend to back home, so I won't be around for a few days. I'll let you know when I get back."

"I understand. But, when you get back, there's no need to stay at the boarding house. You can stay here. I have three guestrooms. You're welcome to use whichever one of them strikes your fancy."

"I'll give it some thought," Cilla said, smiling. Then, she hopped into her Aerostar van and was gone.

CHAPTER 5:
CLUES

Jennifer Baumann was late to work at the Bronson Flower Boutique—not that she was in a hurry to get there. It wasn't that she didn't like the job, but her boss, Dave, was a pain-in-the-butt. She liked working with flowers, and doing the arrangements, but Dave was constantly pointing out one thing or another he didn't like. Jennifer was convinced he did it to annoy her, since her arranging skills were fine. Plus, the jerk thought he was the best thing that had happened to her. He was always leaning too close, putting his hands on her shoulders. Jennifer was just waiting for him to pat her on the rump, so she could deck him. So far, he hadn't tried it, denying her the satisfaction. Just like Dave—anything to be annoying.

Because she was in a hurry, bustling with her purse, fishing for her car keys, Jennifer didn't notice the approach of a furtive figure—until a blow to the back of her skull rendered her unconscious.

Jennifer opened her eyes to total darkness. She blinked a few times to no avail. Either the place she was in was devoid of light, or she was blind. The second two things she noticed, almost simultaneously, were that she was cold and that she was completely naked. She had no idea how long she had been in this place, or in this condition. She reached out all around her but felt nothing, save the cold cement floor. Wherever she was, it wasn't as small as a grave.

When Jennifer opened her eyes again, she was still in darkness — naked, cold, and frightened. Left in this dark place — for how long she didn't know — deprived of food, water, light, and the most rudimentary of comforts, she again fell into an exhausted sleep.

But now, something was different. When she tried to bring her hand to her face, she found that her hands and feet were restrained. She could also feel that she was lying on a cold surface — strapped to a metal table of some sort. She was about to cry out, when some small lights, the sort people used at Christmas, came on overhead. She squinted against even the intrusion of this small amount of light into her dark-blinded pupils. In spite of her predicament, however, Jennifer was relieved she wasn't blind.

Then, a hooded figure, dressed all in black, moved into Jennifer's field of vision. All she could see were the figure's eyes through the ski mask. Judging by the size of the amorphous black shape, Jennifer guessed it was a man.

"Wh...who are you?" she croaked, her voice rough from disuse and a lack of moisture, "Why are you doing this to me?"

The figure remained silent.

Cilla sat in her van, on an insurance stakeout, but fretted over the Bronson case. There were two bodies—one near Bronson, the other near Altoona. Though the police weren't admitting it, Cilla was convinced it was the work of a serial killer. Though there were female serial killers on record, as well as black serial killers, statistics proved that serial killers were mostly white males. So, Cilla narrowed her search to white males, since there weren't a great deal of black people in the area around Bronson anyway.

Since the two bodies were found in two widely separated locations, Cilla wondered if the killer lived in Bronson, or Altoona. Her gut went with Bronson, however, since the first killing had taken place there. Perhaps the killer was being cagey by doing the second victim near Altoona. Serial killers in the past had shown a high degree of intelligence for the most part, which was why they had been able to run up several crimes before capture. In fact, most of them were captured because they left enough clues for the police to follow.

How many women would this particular

killer claim before capture? And, would they all be women? Cilla had another hunch that they would. So far, she didn't have enough information to make any conclusions but she did know one thing — Vint was innocent. Then, why did a little, nagging thought that he could be the killer keep scratching at the back of her skull?

"Who are you?" Jennifer asked again, her voice betraying her terror, "Why am I here?"

Again, the figure didn't speak. He reached up with a surgical-gloved hand, took hold of her right breast, and squeezed.

"Hey! Stop that!" Jennifer shouted, her voice cracking with fear.

Her antagonist responded by clamping his other hand over her mouth, at the same time releasing her breast. Jennifer could smell the rubber of the glove. She felt weight on her thighs. Then, she felt something probe her crotch! Her skin crawled, and she struggled, but her bonds held her fast. Jennifer realized at that moment that she was about to be violated. She screamed into the glove, and struggled with all her might, but was helpless to prevent the assault. Why was she being treated this way — what she had done to deserve such treatment?

Farmer Herman Danzig liked to get an early start to his day. That's why he was out on the road at 5AM, driving his tractor to fields he leased from a neighbor. At this hour, it was also a way to avoid traffic. The last thing he needed was to be leading a conga line of stressed commuters. A tractor wasn't exactly a speed demon. That's why Herman couldn't fail to notice a beat-up van of indiscriminate color pull from the side of the road ahead of him and accelerate away rapidly. Due to the dim light, he didn't see much detail, not even the license plate.

When Herman got to where the van pulled onto the road, he looked into the ditch at the side of the road and noticed a flash of white. He stopped the tractor and stepped carefully onto the soft earth around the ditch. He followed the deep ruts the van made. When he got closer, he discovered the flash of white was the flank of a nude woman lying in the muddy water at the bottom of the ditch!

Jim Fournier's mood deepened as he worked over Jennifer Baumann's body. All the evidence was there — the same contusions and bruises — and in all the same places. Yet, it wasn't the work he performed that sickened him — he was inured to that. This was another murder like the Langsfelder and Stiglitz cases. As far as he was concerned, Jennifer Baumann was the third victim of the same killer — or killers. Regardless of what the police said, it was beginning to look like a serial killer was loose in the area. Jim wondered how many more young women would end up on his examination table.

Susan Kroeger worried over the Baumann case. It was the second murder within the Bronson city limits. Their small town was going to be on the map big time, once the press got a hold of the story. Try as they might, it would eventually be all over the six-o'clock news.

Now, she and Don were going to pick up Vint Montrose for questioning. She hated to be after him again. Personally, she didn't think he was guilty of any of the murders but others at headquarters didn't share her belief.

This was the part of the job she liked least.

Vint was angry. Not only was he angry at being brought in for questioning yet again, but he was angry at the prospect of yet another young woman's murder. Jennifer Baumann was also one of his parishioners — and a loyal one at that. She was among the half-dozen or so who came out each Sunday. Now she was dead. Vint wondered who was preying on the female members of his congregation. He also wondered when Cilla would be back to help him solve the case. The murderer had to be stopped.

When Cilla returned, and knocked at his front door, Vint was so happy to see her he hugged her.

"Gee sailor, I wasn't gone *that* long."

"Sorry...I didn't mean...I was just glad to see you again. So, how long will you be able to stay?"

"Did I say I was going to stay here?" Cilla answered.

"Oh...I just assumed...."

Seeing the deflated look on Vint's face, Cilla decided not to keep bantering. "Look, I was kidding with you. Anyone who leaves his office door open—I mean, I trust your intentions. I'll be happy to stay here. And I wasn't offended, by the way, just surprised."

"You had me going there for a minute, but I'm glad you decided to stay. Oh, while you were gone, there was another murder," Vint said, his countenance grim, "It was Jennifer Baumann, another member of what's left of my congregation."

"Yeah, I know."

"You *do*?"

"Just because I'm not on the scene, doesn't mean I'm deaf and dumb. I'm a detective. It's what I do."

"Touché. So, what's the plan, *detective*."

"I'd like to see my friend Jim Fournier again, then interview some of the good folks of Bronson. But, right now I'm too bushed to do anything. Show me to my room?"

"Certainly, right this way. I'll take your bag and let you pick the VIP suite you like best."

That evening, after Cilla had showered and taken a nap, Vint surprised her with a spaghetti supper. He had gone to a lot of effort, right down to the candles on the table.

"Wow, you do this for all your boarders?"

"Just part of the VIP treatment," Vint said, smiling.

They sat down and conversation was suspended temporarily while Cilla tucked into her meal. Once the initial flurry of eating subsided, Vint broke the silence.

"So, who do you think you'll start with?"

"Well, actually, I already started. I interviewed the Langsfelders shortly before I left." Cilla could see Vint's face fall at the news. "Look, I was sensitive to their pain. And I didn't ask any questions that would embarrass you, if you're worried about that."

"I'm not worried. And I understand you have to interview everyone connected to the case," Vint said, meeting Cilla's gaze.

"Okay—that's settled. Now, getting back to my plans, Becky Langsfelder was found on a back road out near the Smithfield farm. And Jennifer Baumann was found close to the Danzig farm. I thought I'd pay them both a visit and see what I can dig up. This garlic bread is very good, by the way."

"Thank you. Want me to go with you?"

"That won't be necessary—I'll be fine. I'm only going to ask some non-committal questions.

It'll be all right."

"Well, you can understand my concern."

"Yes, and I appreciate it. But, I'll be okay—really. More wine, please?"

When Cilla got home from school she found the front door ajar and the house dark.

"Hello?" she called, "Anybody home?" Silence. "Mom? Dad?"

Cilla entered the house, and checked the rooms on the first floor. Nothing was disturbed, nor was anyone there. She climbed the stairs to the second floor, a sense of dread and foreboding pressing down on her. She felt like the heroine in a cheesy horror flick. The only thing that was different was that she wasn't wearing a flimsy nightie. She got to the second floor and checked the master bedroom, fearing the worst. The bed was made and the room was in order. She checked the bathroom. Nothing there either. Figuring her parents were out somewhere, Cilla went to her bedroom.

The scene that greeted her rocked her back on her heels. Two charred bodies were lying on her bed. Though they both were blackened beyond visual recognition, Cilla *knew* they were her mom and dad. As hard as it was living with them, dealing with their excessive drinking, Cilla could have never imagined, or wished, anything like this happening to them. She stood in the doorway of her room, crying miserably. Then she looked down at herself and found, to her horror, she was wearing nothing but a flimsy nightgown!

Cilla sat bolt up right in bed, wrenched out of her nightmare by the shock of seeing the nightgown. Yet, it wasn't the surprise it first was. She had been having this nightmare off and on for years, so it didn't leave her in a panic. But why now? Usually, it came to her when she was under stress. Yet, she had barely gotten into the case and was essentially loafing through her days at Bronson — she certainly didn't *feel* stressed.

Since Cilla had a long experience with this nightmare, its impact had long ago used up its ability to scare. She fell back on the pillow and was asleep in seconds. When she awoke, the nightmare would barely be a memory.

The next day, Cilla met Vint at the kitchen table. She was dressed in blue jeans and a floral print blouse. "Man, I slept like a baby in that bed. You sure didn't skimp on that mattress. Either that, or it was the wine."

"A little of both, I think," Vint said, smiling.

"Well, I'm off to see Farmer Smith."

"That'd be Farmer Smithfield, I think."

"Picky, picky, picky."

"Well, I'd think a detective would be more aware of such things." Vint looked up at Cilla, a big grin on his face.

"Boy, wait 'till you see my critique of your

next sermon. It ain't gonna be pretty."

Cilla drove to the Smithfield farm in her nondescript Aerostar minivan. It certainly looked that way on the outside — nondescript, right down to the dull paint — and Cilla wouldn't have it any other way. A private investigator needed a vehicle that didn't attract attention during a surveillance. This minivan, with its tinted windows, made the perfect surveillance vehicle. No one gave it a second look. But, the inside was a different story. The van was equipped with a CB radio, a scanner, and a military surplus GPS locator. Stored in the console were a pair of high-powered binoculars and military surplus night goggles. On the floor of the passenger side, a cooler and a couple of insulated travel mugs resided. A small refrigerator resided in the back, along with a hot plate and microwave. There was a Haliburton-style box, securely bolted to the floor in back, that contained a riot-type shotgun, a nine-millimeter automatic, a .357-magnum revolver, a .32 caliber Beretta automatic, and boxes of ammo for each of them. The center row of seats had been removed and replaced with a single, captain-style seat, overhead light, and small table — a handy place to eat or do paperwork. All the locks were upgraded from standard equipment to Ace locks, to insure all this gear stayed inside the van and not in the hands of a thief.

Cilla pulled the van to the side of the road in

a location that afforded a view of the farmhouse and barn. She got out her binoculars and surveyed the scene. During her surveillance, she noticed a man go from the house to the barn. She also noticed a woman leave the house to hang some laundry. Nothing unusual there. Satisfied that things seemed okay, Cilla drove up to the farmhouse. When she knocked on the front door, the woman answered.

"Hello, Mrs. Smithfield?"

"Yes...?"

"My names Cilla Stephenson. I'm a private investigator. I'd like to ask you a few questions, if I may."

"Questions? About what?"

"You may have heard about a young woman who was found near your place?"

Mrs. Smithfield dropped her eyes. "Oh... yes...that poor girl." Then she looked back up at Cilla. "But I don't see how I could be of any help."

"You'd be surprised. Would it be okay if we talked?"

Mrs. Smithfield looked around. "Well, I guess...okay...come in. Do you want me to call Carl in?"

"Would you please?"

Mrs. Smithfield showed Cilla into the parlor and directed her to a seat. Then, she went and called Carl in. The parlor was neat but in the classic old-farmhouse tradition. Mrs. Smithfield and Carl entered the room and he looked at Cilla like she was a stain on the carpet.

This looks like a barrel of fun-in-the-making, Cilla thought. She put her recorder on the table in front of her. "Do you mind if I record this?" she asked, expecting a no, "It helps me to keep track."

"No, it's okay with me," Mrs. Smithfield said, looking toward her husband, "Carl?" He shook his head.

Cilla, surprised by their compliance, tried a couple of non-committal questions to get a feel for the cooperation level of her interviewees. Carl was especially intransigent at first but, put at ease by his wife's cooperation, began to supply some two-word answers. Cilla then tried some more-to-the-point questions.

"The girl's body was found a half-mile from your place. It's pretty quiet out here then, I would guess. Did you hear a vehicle, or a commotion the night before she was found?"

"No, I don't...." Mrs. Smithfield began, then changed her mind. "Wait...I do recall hearing the dogs bark a lot. It's something they don't do often."

"Dogs?"

"We keep three dogs out on the property," Mr. Smithfield cut in, "In warmer weather, we let 'em run. They stay on our land—it's their territory and they guard it."

"Did either of you investigate the cause of their barking?"

"I went out on the property," Mr. Smithfield said impatiently, "Brought my shotgun too, just in case, but didn't see anythin' and went back in. The dogs were quiet after that."

"I see."

"Look, you 'bout done here Miss?" Smithfield said, not bothering to conceal his aggravation at this interruption.

"Yessir. Thank you for your time." Cilla got up and walked toward the front door. "Are you the only ones who live here?"

Mr. Smithfield glared at Cilla, angry at another question. Mrs. Smithfield hastily offered an answer. "Our daughter stays with us when she's home from college."

"She's not here now," Mr. Smithfield added, impatiently holding the front door, "You best be goin'. We got work to do."

Yeah, the place is really jumping, Cilla thought as she exited the house and walked to her van.

Cilla grabbed a burger on her way to Altoona to see Jim Fournier. The medical examiner seemed genuinely glad to see Cilla.

"Thanks for seeing me, Jim. You probably know why I'm here."

"Yes — Jennifer Baumann. Follow me."

Fournier led Cilla to the examination room, where he had Jennifer Baumann lying on a table.

"You were working on her?" Cilla asked

incredulously.

"No, I finished days ago, but brought her out when you called."

"That was nice of you."

"Least I could do for my favorite assistant," Fournier said, giving Cilla a crooked smile.

They walked over to where Jennifer lay and Cilla looked down on her nude form. The classic, stitched-up "Y" incision had been made in her chest, the cut made around the breasts, so as not to bisect them. All cleaned up and past rigor mortis, Jennifer, aside from the paleness of her skin, looked like she might have just been sleeping. Her glossy, black hair was neatly combed and her face, even without makeup, looked peaceful and beautiful—even in death. Cilla realized how appropriate the phrase, "Rest in Peace" seemed at this moment.

"Do medical examiners always take such good care of their charges?" Cilla asked.

Fournier actually blushed. "Not all. I just feel they should be treated with respect. You'll probably think I'm weird, but these girls are so pretty, it just doesn't seem right not to be careful of it—not that I treat the men and older ones with any less respect."

"No, I don't think you're weird. What's weird is the fact that someone else thought so little of her when she was alive."

Fournier looked at Cilla like he had just heard the wisdom of the ages. "You'd have made a good M. E. You've got all the right instincts."

"Thank you," Cilla said, a little non-plussed at the compliment. "To get back to the reason I'm here, were the things you found consistent with the other two victims?"

"Pretty much, but not so much all-over contusions as the other two. The killer might have spent less time with her, so she wasn't in confinement for as long."

"Evidence of rape? Semen traces?"

"Yes — and no — same as the others. This guy's very careful. Must wear a condom."

"Even using a condom, it's next to impossible to avoid leaving a trace. Perhaps he uses other means," Cilla observed darkly.

"You mean a dildo, vibrator, that sort of thing?"

"Uh-huh.   Any   evidence   of   anal penetration?"

"Not that I could detect. And, whatever was used — it was soft. Your assessment seems to be on target. Aside from the bruises on, and around, her mons veneris, there's no vaginal tearing."

"Do you consider that unusual?"

"I guess not, just puzzling. But one thing's for sure. None of the sexual abuse contributed to the homicide. She was strangled to death — plain and simple — just like the other two."

Susan looked up from her paperwork — the ever-present, endless paperwork — and saw Cilla approach her desk.

"Hi Susan," Cilla said airily, "I was wondering if you could fill me in on the Baumann murder."

"Yeah, I figured you'd be here," Susan said, plopping a thin file folder on her desk, "so I put a folder together for you."

"Gee, thanks. That's really nice of you. Does Dad know you're being so helpful?"

Susan offered a chagrined smile. "Well, he told me to help you out."

There was something about Cilla that Susan instinctively liked. Perhaps it was because they were both trying to make it in a man's profession. Perhaps it was Cilla's intelligence—something that was evident right away. Whatever it was, it made Susan want to help her.

"I appreciate it, Susan, I really do. Is Don still looking at Vint?"

"Yeah. I think he's barking up the wrong tree, however. I don't think Vint did either of the murders. It's not like him at all—he's too nice a guy."

Cilla looked intently at Susan Kroeger, noting her solicitousness toward Vint. "You really like him, don't you?"

"Who?"

"Vint."

Susan's eyes narrowed and she gave Cilla her best law enforcement look. "What are you driving at?"

"I'm just trying to establish any relationship

you might have had with Vint."

"For the case, or for your own personal satisfaction? And why do you call him Vint?"

"He's my client."

"Oh? Is that all he is — a client?"

Cilla realized Susan was trying to put her on the defensive, and she was determined not to rise to the bait. "Touché. Okay, did you date *Reverend Montrose*?"

"How is that relevant to the case?" Susan asked, still in 'cop-mode.'

"Come on Susan, it's something they teach you in Interrogation 101. *Everything's* relevant. Putting many small, inconsequential facts together makes a case — you know that."

"No, I didn't date him — not that I'd have turned him down," Susan conceded, "He's a hunk, single, and a good prospect. He just never asked me. There — you get what you want?"

Cilla nodded, turned, and left the station.

Susan watched her go, miffed at Cilla's self-assurance, yet feeling admiration toward her as well. Sighing, she bent once more to her paperwork.

Cilla's next stop was the town garage. Farmer Danzig could wait, she wanted to question the owner, Stuart Loeb, first. Loeb was supposed to have been keeping company with Jennifer Baumann, as well as Becky Langsfelder. She pulled up to the gas pump out front to get some gas. A lanky young man in dirty bib overalls came from out of one of the mechanic's bays, wiping his hands. He smiled when he saw Cilla.

"How do, Ma'am. What can I get you?"

"Fill it up regular, please."

"Sure thing." Loeb started the pump going, then walked back to Cilla's window. She took the opportunity to turn on her recorder. "I've seen this van around here the last couple of weeks but didn't know it was yours. Don't see many Aerostars around these days. Good van. This one's in nice shape too."

"I try to keep up with its maintenance."

"Tinted windows too. Must like your privacy." Loeb turned on what he considered his most charming, lascivious smile.

Cilla figured Loeb for a ladies' man. He was ruggedly handsome, tall and lanky, but slovenly. And it wasn't the fact he was greasy from his work. His general appearance was long-term unkempt. "The van works out well for my work. I'm a private investigator."

Loeb's eyebrows went up. "Private dick, huh?" he said, chuckling at his witticism, "Wouldn't a thought a little thing like you would be in that line a work."

"Interesting choice of words there. I'm not sure *'dick'* would be appropriate in my case," Cilla countered, smiling sweetly, "I prefer the term private *investigator*. It's more professional sounding — less insulting too."

Loeb lost some of his affability. "Didn't mean anything by it. Just a figure of speech, y'know?"

"Anything you say. Actually, I'm here on a case. I'm working for Reverend Montrose."

"The minister? What for?"

"I'm trying to get to the bottom of those awful murders—Rebecca Langsfelder and Jennifer Baumann."

"Ain't the police working on those cases?"

Cilla heard the pump nozzle click off. Ignoring it, she continued. "Yes. You knew Jennifer Baumann, didn't you?"

Loeb seemed a little uneasy. "Yeah, she and me went out a few times. I was real sorry to hear she got...well...."

"I'm sure you were, Mr. Loeb. Would you say you were on good terms then?"

"Yeah—we were kinda cozy, y'know? We kinda hit it off, if y'know what I mean."

"No tiffs, or blowups?"

"No. Me and her—we had a thing going."

"What about Rebecca? You have a thing going with her too?"

Loeb's expression grew surly. "Why are you asking all these questions? You think I killed them women?" Loeb walked back to the nozzle to finish up.

This was a critical point in the questioning. Handle it wrong, and Loeb could get hostile. It was time for Cilla to smooth things out. When Loeb got back, she would need to change tack.

He stowed the nozzle and walked back to her window.

"That'll be fifteen bucks," Loeb said sullenly. Cilla fished out a twenty and handed it to him.

"I wasn't implying anything. I'm just trying to piece together some clues to what happened. I'm sorry if you thought I was accusing you." She tried to look as sincere as she could, avoiding too big a smile.

Loeb looked at Cilla, his anger dissipating somewhat. "That's okay," he said, "I was just feelin' you out. Bronson's a small town. Folks tend to look after one another, y'know what I mean? Tend to get a little wary of outsiders poking around." Loeb teased a five out of a greasy wad of bills and handed it to Cilla.

Cilla took it from him and met his eyes. "Well, somebody didn't look after two of Bronson's women," she said, starting the engine, "Thanks for your help, Mr. Loeb." She put the van in gear and pulled away. *Why do I feel I like need to take a shower?* she thought, glad to be putting some distance between her and Loeb.

Cilla decided to go to Maggie's Diner and catch an early supper before going back to the parsonage. She figured she could kill two birds with one stone. She wanted to question one of the waitresses there—Kathy Lampenmeier— who was a good friend of Jennifer's. Chances are, Kathy would still be on shift. Cilla slipped into a booth and an attractive, brown-eyed, blonde approached. Other than a light tracing of eyebrow pencil on her naturally blonde eyebrows (which wouldn't be seen otherwise), there wasn't another trace of makeup on her pretty face. *Bronson sure has its share of great-looking women,* Cilla thought.

"Hi there," the waitress said, laying a menu and a glass of ice water on the table, "Something to drink?"

Cilla saw that her nametag read *Kathy*. "Unsweetened ice tea please. You're Kathy Lampenmeier, right?"

Kathy had a questioning look on her face, then looked down at her nametag and smiled. "You'd make a good detective. But...how did you know my last name?"

"Actually, I *am* a detective. The name's Cilla Stephenson." Cilla stuck out her hand, which Kathy shook. "I knew there was a waitress who worked here by that name and I made the connection when I saw your nametag."

"Wow, you're a real detective? You work for the police?"

"No, I'm a private detective."

"That must be *so* exciting!"

"It's more day-to-day detail work, but I do love it. Look, do you think you could take a break and talk with me? I'd really appreciate it."

Kathy looked around the diner. There were two patrons and the other was eating. Another bored waitress sat at the counter with a cup of coffee. "It's pretty slow, so I guess so. What would you like to eat?"

"Do you have flounder?"

"Yeah, nice fresh fillets."

"Okay, I'll have the flounder dinner. But hold the potatoes—just some steamed broccoli and some butter. And one of those little dinner rolls. Okay?"

"Sure—sounds good. I'll order up two and tell Blanch I'm taking a supper break."

A waitress named Blanch; go figure, Cilla thought.

Kathy returned after awhile with a tray with their suppers and beverages. She set them on the table, then joined Cilla. They started to eat. Cilla put her recorder on the table.

"Mind if I record our interview?"

"No, not at all. Wow, do all private detectives use those?"

"Not all. I use it to keep a record—so I don't forget small details."

"Ah, that's a good idea. You want to ask me about Jennifer, don't you?" Kathy asked, looking pleased that she had possibly anticipated Cilla.

"Yes, is that okay?"

"Sure, I'm glad to help."

"You were good friends with Jennifer?"

"We literally grew up together—best friends through school, first grade, right through to high school graduation. When I heard how horribly...." Kathy began to tear up.

"Try not to dwell on it, Kathy," Cilla said, laying her hand on Kathy's. "Jennifer went out with Stu Loeb from time to time, right?"

Kathy's expression went from sad to stern. "Yeah, but I told her all the time she could do better. Stu's a real jerk. Thinks he's God's gift, y'know?"

"Yeah, I just had a dose of the old Loeb charm when I got some gas. Did they argue at all?"

"Like cats and dogs. Jennifer came in here all the time, her eyes red from crying. She had a soft spot for stray tomcats like Stu. I told her guys like him would only break her heart. Hey, do you think he…?"

"That's what I'm here to find out. This food is very good. Your cook has a deft touch. I liked the meat loaf I had for lunch awhile back as well. He knows how to put together a solid meal."

"Not he — she. Helen owns the place and does all the cooking. Well, sometimes her son cooks. He's pretty good too."

"Helen? Why isn't this *Helen's* Diner?"

"Helen bought it from the original owner, Maggie. Everyone knew it as Maggie's place and Helen thought it would be bad luck to change the name."

"I see. How old is Helen's son?"

"In his thirties, I guess."

"Does he have a girlfriend?"

"Who — Harry? No. He's a strange looking man — kind of acts strange too."

"How so?"

"Well, he talks to himself all the time. Does all right on getting the food orders straight, but the girls say he gives them the creeps."

"How about you? Does he creep you out too?"

"Nah, I feel kind of sorry for him. He's harmless, as far as I'm concerned — wouldn't hurt a fly. Hey, wait a minute! Harry had a crush on Jennifer. He was always bringing her some kind of special desert. Oh my God…do you think he…?"

Cilla was amused by Kathy's wide-eyed innocent take on things. "Kathy, you have to stop asking that," she said, smiling, "You're beginning to repeat yourself."

"Oh, sorry."

"No problem. What was Jennifer's reaction to Harry's crush?"

"Oh, she was so sweet. Didn't encourage him exactly, but she didn't snub him either. She was always nice to him. Like me, she wasn't put off by his manner."

"Okay, thanks," Cilla said, sliding one of her cards across the table, "Look, if you hear or see anything suspicious, would you let me know?" She made a mental note to talk with Harry.

"Sure. I'd be glad to help find Jennifer's killer."

"Oh, one more thing, if you don't mind," Cilla added.

"Sure thing. What?"

"Did you ever date Loeb?"

Kathy dropped her eyes to look at her hands. "I hate to admit it, but yeah, I did a couple of times."

"Why only a couple of times?"

"It was before he went out with Jennifer. He was a beast."

"A beast? How so?"

Kathy twisted her fingers together, clearly nervous. "He was...I don't know...brutal. Not that he hit me or anything, but I got the distinct impression he was capable of it, you know?"

"So, that's why you broke up then?"

"That, and the fact he didn't seem interested in romancing me."

"What? He wasn't paying enough attention to you?"

"It was more than that. He didn't get busy with his hands, or try to move in for a kiss. We'd go out to supper, maybe take in a movie, but that's it. Listen, I'm as leery as the next girl around pushy guys. You know—they buy you a meal and a couple glasses of wine, then want to jump in the sack? Stu never even tried. Weird, huh?"

"I guess it was," Cilla said, mulling over Kathy's revelations.

When Cilla finished supper, she headed to the parsonage. Vint was sitting in the living room, reading his Bible, when she entered the house.

"Don't you ever watch TV?" Cilla asked.

"Never got into the habit. I do watch once in awhile, though. So, how was the hunting?"

"Pretty good. Met some strange people though. The Smithfields were creepy—like American Gothic via Dean Koontz. I also spoke with Stu Loeb."

"So, are Farmer Smithfield and Stu suspects then?"

"Everybody's a suspect until the facts exonerate them."

"See? That's what worries me. You could be putting yourself in jeopardy."

"Awww, he likes me. Seriously, they didn't realize I was packing heat."

"Is talking like Sam Spade part of the private investigator mail order course?"

"Always with the mail-order thing." Cilla complained, "Yeah, I got the application in the back of a Raymond Chandler paperback novel."

"I'm sorry. I was making a lame attempt at humor. But you do come on kind of macho at times."

"Macho? Me? Just because I use the term 'packing heat?'"

"Well, yeah—since you bring it up. It's not something you'd hear the church deaconesses use in everyday conversation over tea—and folks around here carry rifles in racks in their pickups."

Cilla dropped her eyes. "Perhaps it's a defense mechanism. I was always so 'girly' as a kid—soft and overweight—that I must have decided I needed to toughen up my image later on."

"You don't have to use terms like 'packing heat'—or to toughen up—you're fine as you are."

"Really?"

"Really. You're a capable young woman—good at what she does. Humorous comments about your chosen profession can't change that."

Once again, Cilla felt a strong attraction to Vint. Even when he was apologizing for a gaffe, he managed to win her over. Where had he been all her life?

"You had supper?"

"Huh?" Cilla said, snapping out of her train of thought.

"Have you had supper."

"Yeah, I took the opportunity to eat *and* question Kathy Lampenmeier."

"Was she helpful?"

"Very. She's keeping an eye open. Vint, I have to *find* this guy. Until I do, pretty girls like Kathy are fair game for him. And, speaking of pretty, this town seems to have more than its share of beauties. Do they grow 'em out in a field near here somewhere?"

Vint gave Cilla a shocked look. "Wow, you caught on to us *so fast*! Pretty women are our biggest cash crop. It's a little known secret about Bronson. It's the water, I think."

"Then I'll have to start drinking more of it."

"You don't need to, really."

"Really?" Cilla asked, deliberately fishing for a compliment, "You don't think I need it, huh?"

"I think you're pretty enough, sure," Vint said, dropping his gaze in embarrassment, "but it's more than that. It's *everything* about you."

"Go on, this is beginning to interest me. I'm not letting you off the hook just yet."

Vint met Cilla's eyes once more. "To me, a woman's so much more than the external packaging. Sure, the externals can get a guy's attention, but there has to be more there."

"And I have it?" Cilla asked, surprised at her shameless probing.

"I'm surprised you don't know that. You're smart, energetic, confident, and capable. You don't bank on your looks. You make your mark in other ways."

"Don't be so sure about that 'don't bank on your looks' part. I'm a woman—I know how to work it when I have to. I didn't get left out completely in the looks sweepstakes."

"I'm aware of that. But, it isn't your trump card. Someone only needs to talk with you for five minutes to know you're so much more intelligent than you let on. Then, there's your sense of humor. You use it like a shield."

"Are you sure you don't mean crutch?"

"No, I understand it was developed as a defense mechanism when you were growing up. But you've adapted it to your present condition and use it well. It's one of the things I like about you — that, and the fact you know how to be quiet too."

Cilla went and plopped herself down on the couch next to Vint. "Y'know, you're a pretty perceptive guy. You read me pretty well."

Vint's eyebrows went up. "I didn't see *that* coming."

"Huh?"

"No quip. You were serious that time."

"Well, I couldn't find too much to argue about — or joke about defensively."

Vint looked intently at Cilla. "I think you're getting under my skin. I...."

"Yeah? 'I...' what?"

"I was going to say I...no, it's silly for me to say it." Vint wondered why he was having so much trouble speaking his mind.

"Oh no you don't. Come on, out with it Reverend."

Vint put down his book and looked into Cilla's eyes. "I know it seems too soon, but I think I'm kind of falling in love with you."

Cilla's brows shot up. She was going to let fly with another quip but simply smiled instead. Then she leaned forward and met Vint's lips with her own. In seconds, his arms were around her and they were merging into passion. When that first, long, deep kiss ended, Vint kissed Cilla's freckled nose, her cheeks, and each of her eyes. Then, he pulled her into a hug. Cilla melted up against him, her arms going around his broad back. She could smell the "man" smell of him, mingled with his deodorant and aftershave. It was a good combination of smells. Finally, Vint loosened his hug and she sat up, looking into Vint's eyes.

"If this were one of those romance novels, I suppose this would be where you sweep me into your arms and carry me off to the bedroom."

Vint smiled. "But, this is the parsonage — and I'm the parson. Wrong book."

"Ever read *The Scarlet Letter*?" Cilla turned and sat back, snuggling against Vint.

"*The Scarlet Letter*? Ouch."

"It's considered a romance novel."

"A stern, moralistic romance novel maybe."

"I was just making a point."

"Okay, okay — I concede the point. Can't we just enjoy the moment and not read anything into it?"

Cilla turned her head and looked up into Vint's eyes. "Sure, but any time you want to sit and *not* talk, you just let me know."

"You'll be the first to hear about it."

The next morning, Cilla decided to have breakfast at Maggie's. When she entered the door Kathy Lampenmeier spotted her and waved.

Cilla waved back and took a seat.

"Hi there," Kathy said, "What can I getcha?"

"How about coffee, two eggs, over easy, rye toast, dry, and an interview with Harry."

"Wow! You're in luck!" Kathy said, scribbling Cilla's order on her pad, "He's going to be coming off shift in a half-hour."

"Please let him know I'd like to speak with him."

"Sure thing," Kathy said, winking conspiratorially.

Cilla had just finished with her breakfast, when Harry shuffled over to her booth. Cilla estimated him to be about six-one, but he was so stoop-shouldered, he looked more like five-nine. His features looked almost Mongoloid, like a Downs-syndrome male, but Cilla guessed he wasn't. His complexion was pockmarked and he had a large nose and small, pig-like eyes. As a resident of a town that seemed to have a disproportionate amount of beautiful women, Harry was unfortunately homely.

"Harry?" Cilla asked. He dropped his gaze and nodded. "Please, have a seat. Can I order anything for you?"

Harry shook his head, but slid into the opposing seat.

Cilla smiled broadly when Harry cast a furtive glance her way. "Please don't feel nervous. I only want to ask you a couple of questions." She placed the recorder on the table between them and switched it on. Harry looked at it but said nothing. "You know why I'm here, right?" Again, the silent nod. "Well, let me start by asking if you knew Becky Langsfelder. Did you?" Another nod. "How about Jennifer Baumann?" Ditto. "Okay," Cilla said, her look stern, "Harry, you're going to have to do more than nod at me. I'm not going to be able to get anywhere unless you talk to me. Do you understand what I'm saying?"

Harry nodded, but also said, "Yes'm," in a small voice.

"Good. Now, I need you to be honest with me, okay? Did you really like Becky?"

Harry paused awhile but finally said, "Yes'm."

"Okay, tell me…."

"But she didn't like me," Harry kept going, "Thought I was creepy."

"Did she tell you that herself?"

"No, not exactly. But I could tell."

"I see. What about Jennifer?"

Harry actually smiled. "She was nice to me. She brought me little flower bouquets from her window garden, and donuts from the Dunking-Donut store. I like the cream-filled ones best — the ones with the chocolate. I was sad when I heard she was…she was…." Harry couldn't bring himself to finish.

"Harry, can you think of anyone who would want to hurt either Becky or Jennifer?" Cilla asked gently.

Harry nodded. "Stu. He was mean to Jennifer. And, me too. Calls me a moron. I spit in his food sometimes." Harry cast a panicked look at Cilla. "Please don't tell anyone about that! I never did it to anyone else and I won't do it again!"

"Don't worry Harry — you're secret's safe with me. Tell me, is there anyone other than Stu?"

Harry pondered Cilla's question. "Yeah, there's Mr. Jenks. He's always flirting with the waitresses. But he's old and has dirty hands."

Cilla looked down at Harry's hands. They were immaculately clean and well manicured. "How about Pastor Vint? You ever speak with him?"

Harry's expression brightened. "Yeah, I like him. He's always nice — talks with me and asks me how I am and stuff."

"Do you think he might have hurt Becky or Jennifer?"

"Oh no! He and Becky were lovers," Harry said, then looked like he had said something wrong. "I mean...they were boyfriend and girlfriend. They used to come in and laugh and hold hands — stuff like that. It didn't make me jealous though, 'cause Becky wasn't nice to me." Harry looked around the diner. "Can I go now?

"Yes Harry. Thanks for speaking with me. There, that wasn't so bad, right?" Harry shook his head. "May I talk with you again sometime?"

"Yes'm," Harry answered, hurrying to get up and back to the kitchen.

CHAPTER 6:
HYPOTHESES

Cilla sat in the passenger seat of Susan Kroeger's Explorer. They were riding together, at Cilla's request, to discuss the progress of the murder investigations. In fact, they were headed to Altoona to talk with the detective in charge there, one Dennis Kulpepper.

"This one sure has us stumped," Susan said, "Not one clue as to who the killer might be. Not even a trace of DNA."

"I think law enforcement has grown too dependent on DNA evidence. Think they can't find anything without it. Makes their plain old detective work sloppy."

"Oh, is that so Miss Marple?" Susan quipped, referring to the Agatha Christie female detective, Jane Marple.

"Look, I'm not slamming the police department. But, I have no access to a crime lab and still manage to do my work."

"Not counting Jim Fournier?"

"How'd you know about him?" Cilla asked. Susan blushed. "Ah, I get it—you're an item, huh?"

"Score another for Miss Marple," Susan countered, "Yeah, I've been seeing him off and on for about a year now."

"He seems like a nice enough guy. Serious about his work."

"I know. It's why I like him. He's not the usual, skirt-chasing lunkhead."

"Wow! Hard on men much?"

"With the crop in Bronson, I rest my case—Vint excepted."

"I have to agree with you. I suppose Jim's line of work makes him more sober than most. Are you going to see him today?"

"I was hoping to...." Susan answered, leaving the sentence open-ended.

"Oh, I get it! No problem though. I'll catch a quick lunch—do some sightseeing."

"You—sightseeing? Not much to see in Altoona, I'm afraid. It isn't exactly Philadelphia."

"Well, maybe I can get Detective Kulpepper to spring for lunch."

"He's married."

"All the good ones usually are. Oh well—is there a museum?"

"I think so."

"Good. If not, there's always the library."

"Seriously, you can join us. It's not like we're going to a motel or anything."

"Not that I was implying anything. But I'll cut out at the slightest hint of romance."

Both women had a good laugh over Cilla's quip.

"Detective Kulpepper," Cilla began, "do you have any good leads on the Stiglitz murder?"

"No, I'm afraid we've hit a dead end."

Cilla looked down at the folder before her. Susan had introduced Cilla and requested she be given the relevant facts on the case. Cilla's dealings with Jim Fournier helped smooth the way.

"She was found, lying naked in a ditch about ten miles outside the city limits — right?"

"Yeah, a sharp-eyed motorist spotted her and called us."

"So, it's a pretty sure thing she was transported there. I mean, it was on a main road, right?"

"Yeah. We found tire tracks in the grass on the verge of the road and everything. So?"

"Well, two murders with the same MO were committed in Bronson. So, it's quite possible she was brought from there and dumped in that ditch."

"Anything's possible. But why drop the body here after leaving two in Bronson?"

"Maybe to throw the police off. Have you checked to see if any other murders with this MO have occurred, say, in a one hundred-mile radius?"

Kulpepper frowned at Cilla. "No, we haven't. But it's a good idea. I'll check it out."

Cilla tried hard not to smile when she looked at Susan. Susan gave her a look that said, "Not bad, Miss Marple."

Cilla, Susan, and Jim Fournier lunched together at a Perkins restaurant. The food was good, the décor bright and pleasant, and there were few kids at this time of the day. Cilla noticed the looks that passed between Susan and Fournier. There was definitely something going on there. Cilla decided they made a good couple.

"I'm going to take a walk—work off some of this good food," Cilla said, rising from the table. She fished in her purse, pulled out a ten, and laid it on the table. "This ought to cover my lunch. Let me know if you need more."

"That won't be necessary, Miss Stephenson," Fournier said, "I've got it covered."

"Thanks for the offer, Jim, but there's no need. I appreciate the gesture though. What say I see you back at the station in an hour Susan?"

"Yeah, that's fine. Take your time—even two would be good."

"Two hours it is then," Cilla said, smiling, turning, and walking out of the restaurant.

Out on the street, in the noonday sun, Cilla pondered the theory she brought up to Kulpepper. It was worth checking out. In spite of what he said, she doubted the detective would do the work necessary. TV shows aside, the police were as diligent, or lazy, as anyone else—and just as human.

As she walked along the avenue, Cilla pondered the facts she knew so far. Three murders, two in the Bronson area, one in the Altoona area. Yet, all the victims were dumped by the side of the road. That indicated they were all transported. But where was the killer's base of operations—Bronson or Altoona? Cilla's gut went with Bronson, but she had no way of confirming that.

Then, there were the strange circumstances of the murders. Each woman was strangled to death. That would indicate the killer got off on watching his victim die. There was evidence of a rape in each case but no evidence of semen. The killer could have worn a condom in each case but it still didn't fit. Even with a condom, there would be some evidence of semen. But, since the victims showed evidence of being restrained, he could take his time putting the thing on. that could explain the absence of semen. But still—there was no evidence of pre-coital semen, no lubricant from the condom—nothing at all. Plus, the bodies showed no evidence of being washed.

Finally, there was the "other means" angle. That seemed to fit the best—no evidence of semen, or lubricant. The abuse around the vaginal area seemed consistent with that theory. But why use other means? It just didn't seem to fit for a rapist. They tended to get "up close and personal." Most people mistook a rape for a sexual crime, when it was actually a display of power. The rapist enjoyed his power over his victim — using his penis as a weapon. These murders didn't make sense — unless the murderer was impotent. An impotent rapist? This was an interesting idea but it raised its own share of questions. Was the rapist impotent due to age? Injury? Disease? Physical or mental? If impotent, Cilla could see how he would then get off on the strangling — sort of a deferred sexual release. But why violate the victims mechanically? To inflict humiliation? It almost seemed like two different people were doing the crimes.

The last thought caused Cilla to stop walking, almost causing a collision with the person behind her. Two people? She turned this one over in her mind. If it were two people, the evidence would still hold up and it would explain the seeming dual personality of the murderer. But it wasn't a lock. One crazy man could certainly act this way, for whatever twisted reason. Cilla decided to file this theory for future consideration. She only hoped they would find the killer before another innocent woman fell victim.

Cilla got the idea to visit the Stiglitzes to interview them, so she found a telephone book and looked up their address in the phone book. There was only one entry and the father's first name matched. She called a cab and was on her way. She called Susan on the way to let her know where she was going. She also called the Stiglitz's number.

"Mr. and Mrs. Stiglitz, thanks for seeing me," Cilla said when they answered the door, handing Mr. Stiglitz her card. She noticed that Mrs. Stiglitz's eyes were red from crying and she clutched a limp handkerchief.

"You said on the phone you were working on our daughter's...with the police," Mr. Stiglitz said.

"Yes I am," Cilla said and decided to come clean right off the bat, "But I'm not with the department. I'm a private detective."

Two sets of eyebrows shot up. "Oh?" Mr. Stiglitz said, "Why a *private* detective?"

"I was retained by Reverend Vincent Montrose. As you may or may not know, he's one of the main suspects. The case against him is going nowhere and he's weary of living under a cloud. I was asked to try to get things moving."

"Please, come in, Miss...ah, Stephenson," Mrs. Stiglitz offered.

An identical scene to the one at the Langsfelders was repeated when Cilla found herself sitting across from her interviewees, a cup of tea and her recorder before her.

"I realize this is bad time for you but I guess no time is a good time in matters like this. I'll try to keep my questions brief and to the point. Please forgive me in advance if I cause any pain."

The couple nodded. "Was Amy seeing anyone?" Cilla asked, using the victim's first name to put her parents more at ease.

"You mean, a boyfriend?" Mr. Stiglitz asked.

"Yes."

"Not here—at least as far as we knew."

"What do you mean by that exactly."

"Amy was always running down to Bronson."

"Oh?" Cilla asked, her interest piqued.

"She was seeing that minister of yours," Mrs. Stiglitz put in.

"Vint Montrose?"

"Yes," Mr. Stiglitz answered, "She was on cloud nine about it. She had just started attending his church. Figures. She didn't like our church much—never went, except for the holidays."

Cilla didn't recall seeing Amy at the service she attended. The girl must have been a captive at that time. The thought gave Cilla a chill.

"Did you ever meet Reverend Montrose?"

"No. Amy had just begun seeing him."

"And she wasn't seeing anyone other than Reverend Montrose?"

"Not that we knew. Why are you harping on that? Trying to make our Amy out to be some kind of loose woman for your case?" Mr. Stiglitz said, giving Cilla a hostile look.

"No sir. That's not my intent at all. But Amy was an attractive girl. Attractive girls usually have boyfriends. And boyfriends are suspects in a case like this."

"Amy was a self-contained girl," Mrs. Stiglitz said, "She kept her own counsel. She was always on her computer. We told her she needed to get out more but she didn't listen. We were so happy about her meeting Reverend Montrose, even though he was down in Bronson. We just wanted her to be happy...." With that, Mrs. Stiglitz broke down and sobbed on her husband's shoulder.

Cilla knew she had reached the end of the Stiglitz's desire to answer any more questions. Any further and she would be intruding on their grief over their daughter's death. "Well, that's all the questions I have for now," she said, sliding her card toward the Stiglitzes, "Please call me if you think of anything else. I can find my way out. Thanks again for seeing me at such a difficult time." Cilla retrieved her recorder and hurried out the front door.

Cilla looked at her watch, got out her cellphone, and called Susan. "Sorry to interrupt," she said when Susan answered, "But could you pick me up at the Stiglitz's house? It's at 246 Elm Street. Thanks."

Susan stopped her Explorer in front of the parsonage. "I enjoyed having you ride with me today."

"Look, Susan, you don't have to put a good face on it. I'm just glad you don't hate me for hitting you with those questions a few days ago. Besides, I was a third wheel."

"No, not at all. You were good company. And, you had the grace to leave me with Jim for awhile. We both appreciated it. I'll admit I was a bit steamed at you at first, but I realized you were just doing your job. I should have understood that right off."

"I'm glad to hear that. Thanks."

"Would you mind if I told you something?" Susan asked.

"Not at all. What?" Cilla said, bracing herself for what came next.

"Sometimes you work awfully hard *not* to be accepted."

"Come again?"

"I mean it," Susan insisted, "Why can't you just ease up a bit? What do you have to prove? You're capable, funny, and a great conversationalist. Let people *in* a little."

"Wow, I had no idea you saw me in that way. I don't know what to say."

"Don't say anything. Just think about it— okay?"

"Sure."

"Look, don't go all sullen on me, Cilla. I really like you and consider you a friend already. Deal with it." Susan softened her admonitions by smiling.

Cilla returned her smile. "Okay, I'll work on it. Thanks for the honesty." She reached over, took Susan's hand, and squeezed it. Then, she hopped out of the Explorer, turned, and looked back in. "I enjoyed spending the day with you too—really. You've been extremely helpful. I doubt I'd have gotten as much information as I did, if not for you."

"Hey, we girls gotta stick together," Susan said, chuckling, "Seriously though, I think the department can use all the help it can get."

"Well, I guess we have to adjourn this mutual admiration society, or I'll never get in the house. Good night Susan—see you soon."

"Good night Cilla." With that, Susan put the Explorer in gear and drove off.

Well, that was informative, Cilla thought as she turned and walked to the front door of the parsonage. Troubling thoughts turned over in her head.

When Cilla entered the front door, she smelled cooking. Suddenly, her hunger kicked in. Vint was a good cook—must have paid attention in Home Ec. She walked into the kitchen.

"Hey there, Mr. Prudhomme, what's for supper?"

"Hey, I may have picked up a few extra pounds but…."

"I was referring to your cooking skills. As for your weight, I bet you even have a six-pack."

"That's for me to know and you to find out." Cilla merely looked at him, a serious look on her face.

"Okay, you want to see my six-pack, I'll show you, not that there's anything much to see." Vint pulled up his shirt, revealing a clearly defined set of abdominal muscles.

"See, I *told* you—a perfect six-pack." Cilla observed.

Vint looked down at his abdomen. "Well, I wouldn't go *that* far."

"*I* would. Believe me, growing up as a pudgette, you would rate *way* up there on the 'hunk-o-meter'."

Vint looked into Cilla's eyes. "I'm beginning to see how much your weight as a kid has affected your life."

Cilla's eyes narrowed. "As a kid? What about as an adult?"

"I wasn't passing judgment. I think you look fine. It's obvious you keep yourself fit and watch what you eat. I like you just as you are."

"I was one of a group of 'fat girls' who watched all the thin, good-looking cheerleaders go out with all the hunky guys and get asked to the prom. We commiserated with each other over Twinkies. I finally realized we were living up to a self-defeating paradigm. I put down the sweets, spent more time at the gym, and hit the books. I guess you could say I overcompensated."

"And the captain of the football team asked you to the prom and you drove off into the sunset in his Mustang convertible."

"No. I did get a couple of dates but they were just that—dates—not a ticket to happily-ever-after. What I got was a large dose of independence. I realized I didn't need to rely on anyone but myself."

"So I've noticed," Vint said, realizing the conversation was more an exchange of information than banter between two friendly people.

"What's for supper?" Cilla asked.

"Oh, I see—change the subject."

"Well?"

"Beef stew," Vint said, bending to kiss Cilla on the nose. When Cilla didn't react to it, he looked at her. "What's up—I have bad breath or something?

"What do you mean?"

"You know what I mean. You seem distant, reserved, none of the back-and-forth we usually engage in. Did you have a bad day?"

"Not really," Cilla said walking toward the front door.

"Oh boy, *now* you have me worried."

Cilla decided to drop her bomb. "Why didn't you tell me you knew Amy Stiglitz?"

"Amy?" Vint asked, then continued, "Oh, you questioned her parents today, didn't you?"

"Yeah—and they said she was dating you. Sorry you cooked and all, but I think I'll have supper at Maggie's. Don't like beef stew much."

When Vint entered the diner, Cilla was eating her supper. He went over to her table and looked down at her.

"May I sit down?"

"Sure. It's a public place."

Vint slid into the opposite seat. "Look, I didn't tell you about Amy Stiglitz because we had barely begun a relationship. Quite frankly, with all that's happened, I forgot about it."

"So many clingy girls you can't keep track, huh?"

"Man, how am I supposed to respond to that? Amy was obviously interested but the feeling wasn't mutual. We sat together at the church socials after the morning services—and I took her to supper once after an evening service—but we didn't click."

Cilla looked up at Vint and met his eyes. "Perhaps it's not such a good idea for me to be living at the parsonage. I'll move my stuff out tomorrow morning—stay at the boarding house."

"Why, for Pete's sake?"

"You do the math, Reverend. How does it look, me staying at the house of the guy I'm working for? I should have known better. It isn't professional of me."

"Okay, if that's what you want. But what about us?"

"Us? What *us*? You're a client—that's our relationship. Beyond that...well...."

"Oh, I see," Vint said, dropping his eyes, "I'm still a suspect." He got up. "We can meet at my office if you need to speak with me," he said dejectedly and left the diner.

Cilla watched him leave with tears in her eyes.

Kathy Lampenmeier was late getting out of the diner. It was her turn to close up and, as usual, there was a bigger than normal mess to clean before she could leave. She stood at the back door, fishing around for the keys, unaware she was being observed. A little further down the alley, predator's eyes were fixed on its prey. The culprit was behind Kathy's car waiting for her to approach.

Kathy finished locking the door, and was about to leave, when her cell phone chirped. She got it out and answered it. It was Helen, asking her to get something inside and drop it off at her house on Kathy's way home. Kathy said she would and re-opened the diner with a sigh of frustration. When she reemerged, Susan Kroeger stopped by in her patrol car.

"Everything okay Kath?" she asked, "A little late, no?"

"Busy night," Kathy responded, "and Helen wanted me to get something and bring it to her tonight."

"Sure," Susan responded, "Okay, you go to your car and I'll wait."

"Thanks, but that's not...oh, okay...thanks."

"It's part of my job to look after the good folks of Bronson."

With that, Susan snapped on her searchlight and aimed it at Kathy's car. The black clad figure behind it just barely got under cover in time. Susan waited until Kathy got into her car, got it started, and drove away before snapping off the light.

CHAPTER 7:
FURTHER DEVELOPMENTS

Looking down into the pit, the woman's abductor watched her scuttle away from the light like a surprised cockroach. She looked so helpless and vulnerable in her exposed, naked state, cold, deprived, terrified.

"What do you want with me?" she pleaded, her voice cracking with fear. "Please don't hurt me."

The abductor considered the woman. She was blonde, young, and slender. He liked to see them with more meat on their bones but she was a hasty second choice when the abduction of Kathy Lampenmeier was thwarted.

"Why won't you say something?" the woman asked.

Her abductor responded by lowering a gallon jug of water and some bread crusts in a plastic bag. Soon, she would be on the table, restrained, ready for whatever was to befall her.

Cilla drove out to the Danzig place to interview Farmer Danzig. She didn't hold out much hope that he would further the case, but she had to do the footwork. Sometimes, in asking the routine questions, flashes of inspiration occurred. Cilla couldn't afford to leave any stone unturned.

On the way to the Danzig place, Cilla saw an old granary. A sign on the side of a silo read JENKS' FEED AND GRAIN. Harry mentioned a Mr. Jenks. Cilla then realized the place was between the locations of Becky Langsfelder's and Jennifer Baumann's bodies. Almost before she made up her mind, she found herself turning the steering wheel. She drove up to a decrepit house with a similar sign on the roof, dust roiling out from under her wheels. The place appeared to be deserted. Cilla put the van in park and got out, tucking her revolver in its clip-on holster into the small of her back, hooking it onto her belt.

Before she took a step, the screen door creaked open, startling her.

"...I help you?" a large, grungy-looking, bearded man asked, stepping out of the house. Cilla figured him to be in his late fifties under all the grime. A strong smell of unwashed body wafted in her direction.

"Uh...hi, I'm Cilla Stephenson, she said, switching on the recorder in her pocket. I'm a private investigator, working on solving the murders that have been happening around here. I noticed your place is equidistant between the sites where the two bodies were found, so I thought I might ask if you saw anything." Judging from the reaction she got at the Smithfield place, Cilla figured this guy's reaction would be the same.

"I read about them murders. A real shame — them pretty girls gettin' killed like that. How can *I* help you though?"

Cilla was emboldened by the friendly reception. "Well, did you hear, or see, anything out of the ordinary — a car in the middle of the night, a dog barking — that sort of thing?"

The man smiled, revealing a set of rotten teeth. "Wow, look at me. I get a visitor and don't show a lick of hospitality. Can I get you a sody-pop or somethin'?"

"No, thanks, Mr....?"

"Jenks — but you can call me Phil."

"I just had lunch," Cilla lied, "Can you help me...Phil?"

"I don't remember hearin' or seein' nothin' out of the ordinary. Course, we're pretty far off the road. And I sleep like a log. You could prob'ly hear me snorin' all the way out there."

"I see. Does anyone else live here? Maybe they heard something?"

"Nope. I been livin' here alone ever since Emma — she was my wife — died."

"Sorry to hear about your loss, sir. Thanks for your help." Cilla turned toward her van.

"Weren't much help, I'm afraid. Sure you don't want to come in for a cup a tea or somethin'?"

"Thanks Phil, but I have another interview. You take care now."

"You got a card or somethin'? I could give you a call if I hear anythin' — or remember somethin'."

Cilla took a card from the holder in the dash and walked over to hand it to Phil. "My cell number's on there. You can call me on that anytime."

"Will do," he said, looking down at the card, "...Miss Stephenson. Stop by anytime. Don't get too many visitors these days — ever since the big boys pretty much put me out of business."

"I'll keep that in mind," Cilla said, climbing into her Aerostar, in a hurry to leave the creepy Jenks place.

Out on the road, Cilla pondered what had just transpired. Though Jenks was a grungy, creepy looking guy, right out of the movie *Deliverance*, he had been friendly enough, if a bit over-zealous with his hospitality. Cilla chalked it up to loneliness. Next stop, the Danzig place.

On the way over, Cilla got Susan on her cellphone. "Hi Sue. I wonder — could you help me with something?"

"Sure. What do you need to know?"

"What can you tell me about a Mr. Jenks, of Jenks' Feed and Grain?"

"Oh, him. He's a creepy old guy — the type the local kids like to harass on Halloween. There are rumors he and his daughter are cannibals."

"Daughter?"

"Yeah, he lives there with her. His wife died a few years back."

"Hmmm, he said he lives alone."

"Maybe his daughter died. Didn't ever see her, except from a distance, when I drove by. They pretty much keep to themselves and don't bother anybody. The old man comes into town every so often to buy supplies. Usually stops at Maggie's for lunch, sometimes supper. The waitresses say he creeps them out. And, he smells."

"Yeah, tell me about it."

"Did any of what I gave you help? What were you doing out there anyhow?"

"I saw the sign on the way to the Danzig's and paid him a visit."

"Think he's a suspect?"

"They all are—until they aren't," Cilla quipped, "Thanks for the help. See you soon."

The woman's abductor looked down along the length of her nude body on the table. She had been properly cowed by her time in the pit and merely sobbed softly. She looked up, fear and questioning in her eyes.

"What are you going to do to me?" she asked piteously.

Her abductor wasn't beyond being moved by her plight. She looked so vulnerable, so frail, lying there on the table. The very sight of her caused a pang in his heart. But she was not for his use—yet. He raised a gloved hand and clamped it over the woman's mouth as another black-clad, hooded figure moved to the table.

The woman was for his companion. Once his companion was through, the woman would be his to dispose of. He got no satisfaction from sex any more. Only when he had his hands on the woman's neck and crushed her windpipe, watching the life leave her eyes, would he find release. But, that would have to wait until his companion used the woman. This part was difficult for the abductor. His companion was brutal, unforgiving, heedless to the pain that was the inevitable result of what would take place. He viewed his part as a mercy, releasing the woman from this world of pain and suffering.

Farmer Danzig certainly wasn't from the Smithfield School of Inhospitality, but he wasn't exactly a glad-hander either. He turned out to be a big, tall, classically blonde man of distinctly German ancestry, who wouldn't look out of place as a skiing instructor. He invited Cilla into the house, where his equally tall and blonde wife, as lean as a whippet, served lemonade and homemade gingersnaps.

Cilla sat on a small sofa in the parlor, ate her gingersnaps, and sipped her lemonade in a room so silent it could double as a sound studio. The loudest sound was the chirring of the cicadas outside. Mr. and Mrs. Danzig were of the "don't speak unless spoken to" school. They sat there, calmly watching Cilla until she took one last sip of her lemonade and put it down. She switched on her recorder.

"These gingersnaps are delicious, Mrs. Danzig," Cilla said, "You'll have to give me the recipe."

Mr. and Mrs. Danzig reacted by calmly staring at Cilla, who was becoming decidedly uneasy from this judicial scrutiny. They were beginning to look like another "American Gothic" painting—"*American Gothic, Seated.*" She decided to begin her interview. There was enough silence on the recording already.

"I'm sorry to bring up what must be a horrible memory, but I wonder if I could ask you a few questions about your discovery of the body." Farmer Danzig showed his emotion by staring at her. Cilla figured she might get further by actually asking a direct question. "What was the position of the body when you found it?" Cilla asked. She already knew the answer from the police photos but threw it in as an icebreaker. It worked.

"She was lying sorta face down, but on one hip," Danzig answered.

"I see. Did she appear to have any wounds or bruises?"

"No, not that I could see. It was still pretty dark, with the sun just clearing the horizon."

"What can you tell me about the van?" Cilla asked, then realized she should be more specific if she expected an answer. "Were there any features that stand out in your memory about it?"

"Only that it was pretty beat up, kinda rusty, with primer spots all over it."

"What was the primary color?"

"Y'know, now that I try to recall, I'm not sure. All I can come up with is some sort of gray. But, like I said, it was still pretty dark out."

"Could you see the license plate?"

"No, it was too dark."

"Can you recall ever seeing the van before?"

"No."

"I did," Mrs. Danzig offered.

"You did?" Cilla asked, surprised, "But you weren't with your husband that morning, were you?"

"No, but I've seen a van that matches Herman's description, going up and down the road in the middle of the day."

"Really. Over a long period, or just recently?"

"Oh, about six months back for awhile, but not recently."

"You didn't happen to get the license plate number did you?"

"No, our house is kind of far from the road. But, I think it belonged to the Pastor."

"You mean, *Pastor Montrose*?" Cilla said, floored by the revelation.

"Yes, I remember seeing it parked behind the church a time or two."

"But, your husband said he never saw it."

"He's not much of a churchgoer," Mrs. Danzig said, casting a look over at her husband, who countered with a stern glare.

Pondering this bombshell, Cilla wanted to end the interview. "Well, thank you both for your time. And thanks for the delicious cookies, Mrs. Danzig. Mind if I take a few with me?"

"Certainly," Mrs. Danzig said, "Wait, I have something else for you." Cilla watched as she walked into the kitchen and returned. She handed Cilla an index card. "It's my recipe for the cookies."

"Why, thank so much, Mrs. Danzig...."

"Inga, my name's Inga."

"Thank you, Inga. It's very kind of you." Cilla fished a card out of her pocket. "Here, take my card. You can reach me on my cellphone if you think of anything else. Thanks for the recipe — and the cookies."

Out in her van, munching a cookie, Cilla was reassessing her opinion of the folks around Bronson. Thanks to the Danzigs, she had, besides a cookie recipe, two witnesses to seeing the van — and its owner. She couldn't wait to ask Vint Montrose about it.

Cilla found Vint in his office, bending over his Bible, working on that week's message. He was dressed in running shorts and a basketball tee — it was obvious he was going to go jogging, since he didn't look like he had worked out yet. Cilla thought he looked delectable, but suppressed the thought.

Vint looked up when she knocked softly on the doorframe, since the door was open. "Oh, hi," he said, smiling, "How'd the interviews go today?"

"Fine," Cilla said, her face serious.

"Oh, I see," Vint said, his smile fading, "It's going to be all business. What can I do for you?"

Cilla couldn't think of a way to gracefully ask her question, so she dove right in. "Do you own a van?"

"A van? No. Why do you ask?"

"I just came from the Danzig place. Nice folks."

"A little friendlier than the Smithfields, I suspect."

"Uh huh. The interview went quite well. Mrs. Danzig told me she might have recognized the van the killer used to drop off the last victim's body."

"That's great news—a solid lead," Vint said, putting down his pen and smiling up at Cilla, "Did she know who owned it?"

"Yeah, she did."

"That's great! Who?"

"There's no guarantee it's the same van her husband saw that morning, but she said it looked like one she knew you drove."

Vint's brows knit together. He laid both hands

on the desk. "Wait a minute, I thought you said the body was found by *Mr.* Danzig."

"She recognized it from the description her husband gave." Cilla remembered the paper bag of cookies she was carrying and stepped over to the desk to deposit them there. "Want a cookie? Mrs. D makes great gingersnaps. You can have one while you explain to me why she saw a van that she said you owned."

Vint pulled the paper bag close, opened it, and smelled the aroma that wafted out. "Ummm, smells good," he said, reaching into the bag to retrieve one. He bit into it, closing his eyes in appreciation of the taste, then looked up into Cilla's stern gaze. "These *are* good," he said simply.

He wondered if Cilla were carrying one of her weapons, to come into his office alone to confront him. "As it so happens, I *did* own a van. It was a nondescript piece of junk I got for a couple of hundred bucks. I used it to run errands for the church—you know, back when I actually had a ministry here. Took folks to picnics, hauled food and clothing for charitable work—that sort of thing." Vint took another bite out of his cookie, adding to the crumbs on his lips.

Cilla noticed he didn't lick them off. Was he trying to drive her crazy? All she wanted, at that moment, was to lick them off herself and merge into a long, sweet kiss. She shook off the fantasy by asking a question.

"*Did* own?"

"Yeah. It was stolen about six months ago. Why anyone would want a run-down old thing like that is beyond me. It ran pretty well though. You think it's the van the murderer used to drop off his victim's dead bodies." Vint didn't phrase it as a question.

"Yeah, I do," Cilla responded.

"And you thought it might be connected to me and the murders."

"Yeah."

Vint's eyes narrowed. "Just doing your job, right?"

"Something like that," Cilla said, returning Vint's intense gaze.

"Are we done here then?"

"Yeah," Cilla said, turning and walking out of the office.

As she walked through the doorway, Vint thought he could see the bulge of a holstered gun in the small of Cilla's back, under her blouse. *Another question answered*, he thought.

Out in her van, Cilla's mind raced as fast as she was going on the road. A hundred thoughts ran through her mind, churning there since Mrs. Danzig had mentioned recognizing the van. She hadn't known what to expect when she went to Vint to confront him with the evidence. For his part, he had remained calm—almost too calm—just the way a guilty man would act if he had good nerves. In fact, his *lack* of a reaction was damning in itself. No laughing about it; no pleading with her; no firm declarations of innocence — all of that could be incriminating in itself. Vint had acted the same way when she confronted him with the news about Amy. So calm, so rational, so off-handed about it.

Cilla ran what she knew of Vint through her mental filter and compared it to what she had gleaned so far about the killer. Could Vint be the killer after all? His inviting her to stay at the parsonage could be a way of disarming her, keep her close, and put her at ease.

Then she thought of how sensitive and caring he seemed to be when they had talked. More and more, she had let down her defenses, let him come close. Cilla realized then that she had begun to fall in love with Vint. The thought he might be a murderer caused a chill to run down her spine. She wondered if it was fear — or the thrill of being with a dangerous man.

"What should I *do* Susan?" Cilla pleaded.

Susan Kroeger sat across from Cilla at Maggie's. Two coffee mugs sat on the table between them, along with the pot on a trivet. Cilla had called her to discuss recent findings in the murder investigations and the conversation naturally led to Vint's relationship with Amy and what she had found out about his van. Susan noticed Cilla's agitation when she related her findings. It was obvious Cilla was fond of Vint.

"Well, you know the evidence is entirely circumstantial against Vint. It comes down to whether you believe he did it or not. What does your heart tell you?"

"I want to follow my heart, but I'm a detective. I can't let feelings cloud the issue."

"I've known Vint since he first came here to pastor the church. As I told you, I even hoped he'd ask me out, but it never happened. In all the time I've known Vint he's always come across as sincere and unassuming. He's modest about his looks and is unfailingly courteous. I'm a pretty fair judge of people and he comes across as a solid citizen in my book."

Cilla looked into Susan's eyes, as if searching for answers there. "What about Amy Stiglitz?"

"I don't know much about that. I saw her a few times at services and noticed her with Vint afterward." Susan smiled. "I remember I was a little jealous of Amy for that."

"What was Vint's manner toward her?"

"He was friendly, but formal. No easy manner, loud laughing, casual touching—the sort of things a guy does when he's on the make."

Cilla thought of how easy Vint was with her. Was it because of love, as he said, or to soften her up for the kill? "I'm torn Susan. I'll admit I was starting to fall for him—then I find out two things in quick succession. I moved back to the boarding house."

"Yeah, I know."

"You do?"

"I'm a cop. It's my job to know things."

"I should never have stayed at the parsonage. It's not professional."

"I won't argue with you there. But, there's this wall between you now. Will it affect how you work for him?"

"I honestly don't know."

Susan studied her friend and colleague. Cilla looked as forlorn as a street waif selling flowers. Lines of worry were etched into her forehead. Susan's heart went out to Cilla.

"Look, this is free advice, so make of it what you will. You want to stay in the boarding house? Fine. Can you trust Vint? I say, yes. But...only your heart can tell you what's true about him in the end, even given all the facts. If it's any comfort to you, I'll be there, watching your back."

Cilla looked into Susan's eyes. She reached out to lay her hand on Susan's. "Thanks...thanks for being...my friend."

When Cilla got back to the boarding house, it was nearly midnight. As she walked up the walk, the sight of Vint, who was sitting on the front steps, jolted her. She debated just brushing by him without speaking, when Vint changed the plan by speaking himself.

"You were out late. You're usually an early-to-bed type."

"I had some things to do. I spend a lot of

time with Susan Kroeger, discussing the case. Afterwards, we hung out—sort of a girl's night out. I guess we lost track of time."

"I understand you wanting to move out," Vint said calmly, rising from his seat on the step, "It *is* more professional. I also understand the fact that I once owned a van that could have been used in a series of murders must have come as a shock, as did the Amy revelation. You're trained to consider *all* the facts of a case after all—you wouldn't be much of a detective if you didn't."

At that moment, Cilla made up her mind. She met Vint's eyes with her own. "I've been in an agony of indecision for the past couple of days. First one revelation, then another on its heels. They really shook me up."

"I know," Vint said softly, "I didn't mention the van being stolen because I didn't think it had any bearing on the case, if that helps any."

"The reasoning half of my brain tells me one thing, my heart another," Cilla continued.

"And what does your heart tell you?" Vint asked.

Cilla's face scrunched into the beginning of a good cry, but she managed to reign in her swelling emotions. Then she surprised Vint, and herself, by rushing to him, almost bowling him over by her hug.

"Oh, Vint! I think I started to fall in love with you the moment you answered the door at the church."

Vint could tell by her shaking that Cilla was crying. He lowered his lips to kiss Cilla on the top of her head. The softness and fragrance of her hair were intoxicating. "And I thought you were the most interesting woman I had ever met. The falling in love part came easily after that."

Cilla raised her head to look up at him. "Really?"

"Do you think I give my heart easily?"

"No," Cilla sniffled, "I don't think that."

Vint smiled. "Your detective skills are impeccable." Cilla, her face wet with tears, managed to smile back. "Does this mean you trust me?" he asked.

Cilla nodded. "I certainly seem to have a knack for soaking your shirts," she said.

"No problem—they're easy to wash."

Cilla stepped back and looked into Vint's eyes. She saw nothing there but the same, warm gaze that had won her heart. She made up her mind that what she saw was the truth, and that, whatever happened, she would trust Vint from now on.

Vint put a period on the sentence of her resolve by reaching out, pulling her to him, and bending to kiss her. It was as if a spark coursed through her body. She melted against him, her arms going around his neck, losing herself in that kiss. When they reluctantly broke it off, Cilla was breathing heavily.

"If you weren't a preacher, I'd invite you up

to my room, start tearing your clothes off, and let you have your way with me. Do preachers ever succumb to the call of the flesh?"

"Some do, but not this one."

"Darn — just my luck — you're a straight arrow through and through."

"Will you settle for breakfast at Maggie's tomorrow morning?" Vint asked, "I'm not made of stone, you know."

"Just my luck," Cilla answered, wiping her eyes with her sleeve, "I offer myself to you and all I get is breakfast."

Vint and Cilla sat at a table at Maggie's, their hands around hot mugs of coffee. They had sat in companionable silence for the past fifteen minutes. Now, Cilla broke that silence.

"I think part of my concern over you is that I know so little about you."

"And...?"

"Well, you're such a good listener, you got me to blurt out my entire sordid upbringing. I told you things I haven't shared with anyone other than my best friend."

"Well, aside from the fact I'm a good listener, I doubt that you've told me *everything.*

"Yeah, but you've told me *nothing* beyond your part in the Langsfelder case."

"I'm afraid there's not much to tell. I've had a pretty boring life, really."

Cilla reached out and laid her hand on Vint's.

"Vint, I'm in love with you. Why would I find *anything* about you boring? You weren't *born* a minister. Where did you go to school? What did you want to be when you were a kid? See what I mean?"

Vint dropped his eyes and looked down at his hand with Cilla's on top of it. He placed his other hand on top of hers. The tenderness of the gesture both touched Cilla's heart and caused a pang of suspicion. She felt as if Vint were hiding something.

"I grew up in Northern New Jersey. My Mom and Dad divorced when I was twelve—irreconcilable differences, I think the term is. My Mom had primary custody and I saw Dad every other weekend.

"I hated that they divorced. I acted out like so many other kids whose parents divorced. My grades fell in school. I hung with the wrong crowd, got into trouble at school and with the police. Nothing big—just enough to break my mother's heart. Dad didn't supply any real guidance—tried to be my bud.

"But, there was one thing I excelled at when I go to high school. I was a pretty talented athlete. One of the coaches saw my raw talent and made the decision to work with this rebellious, antisocial kid. He put me on the varsity football team, and on the baseball team. He even tried me at basketball. I did okay, but my heart wasn't in the game. But football and baseball were my loves.

"Coach Ray encouraged me to get my grades up and keep them up, so I could continue to play. The school had a rule that athletes had to maintain at least a C. Coach got me to give him Bs.

"As good a coach as he was, Coach Ray had more going for him. He was a committed Christian. He was careful not to cross the school administration on that score, but he was always there for me when I needed to talk. And he shared his faith too. He became more of a father to me than my own dad. It wasn't long before I idolized him, try as he might to discourage it.

"By the time I graduated high school, my life had changed course. I was a top student, a varsity athlete, and a Christian myself. Coach's patient testimony got through to me and I came to believe as he did.

"Coach got me a full ride scholarship to a solid Christian school in the Midwest. I lettered there and wanted to go into teaching. I wanted to be a coach like Coach Ray." Vint stopped his monologue and looked into Cilla's eyes. "Have I bored you to tears yet?"

"Are you kidding? Boring? Your story sounds like a chapter of *Jack Armstrong, All-American Boy.*"

"How would *you* know about Jack Armstrong?"

"I told you I was an avid reader."

"You did?"

"Well, I was. Spent about as much time in the library as the librarian."

"Oops, there you go spilling your guts again."

"Yeah, you're right. Sneaky. Get me talking and off you. Uh, uh, uh — keep talking mister!"

Vint smiled and took a breath. "I probably would have gone into coaching, but two things happened. The first was that my parents must have been listening to my eager testimonies of my faith. My mom, then my dad, gave their lives to Christ.

The second — though they both had significant others — was that they remarried. An offhanded comment at the wedding reception got me to thinking. Dad was talking to some Christian friends in my presence and said, 'Vint should be a minister. Look how his testimony changed our lives!' It stopped me in my tracks and I thought about it until I graduated college. Then, I enrolled in seminary to become a pastor. The rest, as they say, is history. So, finally bored yet?"

"Not in the least. Your story is anything *but* boring. Hearing it, any doubts I may have had about you are as dead as yesterday's news. Wow! Who would've thunk!"

"Well, it's getting late," Vint said, looking at the diner clock, "We'd best be going."

"Uh, about those comments I made earlier...."

"What comments?"

"You know, about us getting it…uh…."

"Oh, *those* comments," Vint said, smiling, "Look, I'm not offended. I'm a flesh-and-blood man, not some religious icon. I was flattered by your interest — *really*."

Cilla sighed. "Thanks. Still, I meant every word I said, however 'fallen-woman' they may have sounded."

"I know you did," Vint said, standing. Cilla stood as well. Vint walked around the table and took Cilla's hands in his. "And I don't consider you a fallen woman."

Cilla went up on her toes and kissed Vint on the cheek. Then, she turned and practically flew to the diner's exit — leaving Vint with the check.

CHAPTER 8:
MEDIA CIRCUS

REVEREND'S VAN LINKS HIM TO MURDERS!

The paper's headline screamed its lurid news.

"Oh, *this* is just great!" Vint complained, as he picked it up from the front porch. A mob had formed outside the front door, even at this early hour.

"That's him!" Vint heard, as he closed the front door.

Vint turned on the TV and found his story on all the local cable channels, a couple of the Networks, Fox News, and CNN. He reached for the telephone and dialed the local police station. "I'd like to speak with Susan Kroeger, please. Vint Montrose." Another pause, as the dispatcher connected him through to Susan's radio. "Hi Susan. Look, can you get over here and do something about this mob scene on my front lawn?"

"There isn't much I can do, past moving them

off the property. The press, due to their First Amendment rights, has a right to be there."

"It's wonderful how the First Amendment can be used to harass people," Vint said bitterly.

"Well, if you had a beef with some large corporation, or organization, you'd be glad to have their involvement."

"I see your point. Okay. Anything you *can* do would be appreciated. Thanks."

Just then, the doorbell rang. Vint went to the door and opened it. A woman TV reporter stuck a microphone in his face.

"Reverend Montrose, would you like to comment on the accusations?"

Vint looked at the eager young woman, who had been so bold as to go up and ring his bell. He sighed and stepped out onto the porch. He then walked down to where the bulk of the reporters stood. The woman followed him, sticking the microphone out in front of him like someone dangling a carrot on a stick. *They're just doing their jobs*, he thought to himself, trying to remain calm.

Vint held up his hands to still the tumult of shouted questions and to fend off the forest of projected microphones thrust in his direction. The crowd fell into silence.

"Look, I came out here for two reasons. One is to answer your questions. The other is to ask you all a favor. *Please* have some respect for my privacy. You can't continuously be camping out in my front yard." Vint looked at the young woman who had rung his doorbell. "To answer your question, yes, it is my van. But it was stolen six months ago. I also realize that it might have been involved with a murder."

"Haven't you been under investigation by the police for a number of murders?" someone Vint couldn't see shouted.

"Yes, but no charges have been filed. That's because I'm inno...."

"Didn't you date one of the victims — Becky Langsfelder?" the first young woman asked.

"Yes, I did. But we had broken up long before she was killed."

"Was it on bad terms?"

"No, we were still fr...."

"Is it true you have a history of violent behavior?" someone else shouted from the rear of the crowd of reporters.

"Where did you hear that?" Vint asked, looking for the owner of the voice, shocked by the accusation, "I've never hit anyone in my life, outside of a scuffle or two when I was a kid in school."

"Were you suspended, or expelled?"

Vint sighed. "Look, I don't know where you're getting you information from, but no, I wasn't suspended or expelled. It was a different world back then — less fraught with sinister intent. It was merely a schoolyard dustup."

"Is it true you hired a private investigator?"

yet another voice asked.

Vint looked at the man. "Yes, she's helping the police investigate the...."

"Are you sleeping with her?"

"No, I'm not," Vint retorted, his anger rising at the intrusiveness of the question, "She's staying elsewhere."

"Where?" another female voice chimed in.

"Look, I didn't come out here to discuss my private life. I merely wan...."

"Did you hire her to get the police off your back?" another male voice asked.

"Where's she staying?"

"Have you been accused of the other murders?"

Just then, Susan's Explorer pulled up and she got out with a bullhorn.

"Okay folks," she yelled, her voice bellowing through the amplification, "You're on private property! Move back to the street!"

Vint took the opportunity to head for the house.

"Looks like tiny Bronson has hit the map," Susan said when she entered the house later.

"Coffee?" Vint asked.

"Yeah, that'd be great."

"Sorry to cut out and leave you to the mob," Vint apologized.

"Not a problem. I just barked orders and put my hand on my gun. They behaved. It's one of the advantages of being a small-town cop. You can get away with a little gun-waving."

"Is it going to be like this from now on?" Vint asked, a worried look on his face.

"Just for a few days."

"If it gets too bad, does your small-town advantage include shooting a few reporters?"

Susan laughed. "Look, they'll get bored soon and lose interest. Then they'll move on," she answered.

"Yeah, unless another murder occurs," Vint added.

"Aren't you just a little ray of optimism."

"Just a realist."

The abductor walked from the place where the girl was. He wasn't interested in hanging around to watch what transpired. His companion's predilections didn't interest him in the least. He wasn't satisfied by the sexual any more—he had *other* means of release. He would return shortly to do what had to be done.

He walked to where the van was parked in its shed. He would have to ditch it after this drop-off. He figured an auto wrecker in Altoona would be the best place. It would probably be crushed for scrap metal. He'd have to screw up the engine, which ran well, so the salvage yard owner wouldn't try to do some work on it and sell it again. Or, he could ditch it in the river. He also considered a third option. Whatever he decided, its usefulness to him was at an end.

The next morning, the phone at the parsonage rang. Vint took the call.

"Hello?"

"Vint, it's Susan."

"They found another body this morning, halfway to Altoona."

"Oh, man…."

"Not only that, it was in a van at the side of the road. They think it's yours."

"You're going to pick me up, right?"

"For what it's worth, I'm not happy doing it."

"Thanks for that. Are you going to let Cilla know?"

"Already did."

The abductor watched as the police worked in and around the van. The coroner had come to take the girl's body to the morgue, where they would violate her after death still further. What he did to end her pain seemed to him to be the least of her insults.

He had decided to leave the van for the police to find. Before he left it, he went to a do-it-yourself car wash two hours before dawn and hosed it down, inside and out. Then, he went to the church, making sure he drove it around in the dirt on the property. Finally, he rolled it head on into a ditch at the side of the road more than halfway to Altoona.

He walked to a good vantagepoint on a hill a quarter-mile away and settled in with his coffee and donuts until a motorist found the van. As it turned out, it was a local sheriff's deputy.

When the police came for him, Vint was dressed and ready. As soon as he heard about the van, he knew they'd want to bring him in for questioning again. Cilla had wanted to accompany him, but he insisted she go with Susan to find out what she could about the case. Cilla reluctantly agreed and Susan took her to Altoona to meet with the medical examiner. A second car came with her to pick up Vint.

"I hate leaving you like this," Cilla said.

"Don't worry about me," Vint said, with a wry smile, "I'll be in the hands of Bronson's finest." He stooped to give Cilla a quick kiss.

"You understand why we brought you in, Reverend Montrose," Detective Don Franzer said, "We find a van you say was stolen over six months ago. It's obvious that it's been cleaned, but dirt from around your church was found in the tire treads. Not only that, but there are tracks all over the churchyard that match the van's."

"Doesn't it seem odd to you," Vint pointed out, "that someone would go to the trouble to clean a vehicle so thoroughly, yet overlook an obvious thing like that?"

"Did you, Reverend?"

Vint glared at Franzer. It was one of those "Do you still beat your wife?" questions.

"Right this way, ladies," Jim Fournier said, directing Susan and Cilla into the autopsy room.

"I must say, I've been getting a lot of visits of late — not that I'm complaining." Fournier smiled at Susan.

They walked to where the corpse was laid out on one of the stainless steel tables. Fournier had already done the Y incision, and the ribs had been cut, so the chest was laid open, revealing the lungs and other internal chest structures.

Even though she had witnessed a previous autopsy, Cilla's stomach lurched when she saw the woman's breasts laying face down on the table next to the body, attached to their flaps of skin. It seemed like such a violation of the body, even though intellectually, she knew the woman was dead, and beyond insult. Cilla looked over at Susan, noting the grim look on her face and her clenched jaw muscles.

"What's the woman's name, Jim?" Cilla asked.

"Digiamo, Angela Digiamo," Fournier answered after consulting his clipboard. "Sorry you have to see her like this, but autopsies aren't pretty. Should have thrown a sheet over her I guess — not used to visitors.

"It's okay," Cilla said.

"Same MO?" Susan asked.

"Yes, death as a result of strangulation. By the position and size of the bruises, I'd say it was the same pair of hands too."

"Oh man — if this gets out...." Susan groaned, not wanting to finish her thought.

"I don't see how it won't now," Fournier said, "This is the second in the Altoona area. When the media looks at the two from the Bronson area together with Altoona...."

"It'll be a serial killer media circus," Cilla finished for him.

"Precisely," Fournier agreed.

Susan just rolled her eyes.

When Vint got back to the parsonage early the next morning, Cilla was sitting at the table next to the kitchen window with a cup of coffee, looking out into the yard, and listening to her interview recordings.

"My, but you're a sight for sore eyes," Vint said, "How'd you get in?"

"I used your hidden key," Cilla said, switching off the recorder.

"You knew where it was?"

"Like I couldn't figure out it was under the fake rock. I *am* a detective, after all."

"I guess it was pretty obvious at that. You get any inspiration from listening to those recordings?"

"It's why I'm so adamant about making them.

Sometimes I pick up a comment, or an inflection, that can say more than the words do."

"Hmmm," was all Vint could say. He was impressed by Cilla's thorough competence.

"You're pretty chipper for someone who just spent the night in jail," Cilla observed.

"It's not so bad," Vint fibbed, "It's beginning to feel like a home away from home. My back's even getting used to the cot."

"It *was* your old van, wasn't it?"

"Yeah. Even had dirt from around the churchyard in its treads and there are tire tracks there that match them."

"Wow. Someone's really trying to set you up."

"I don't think so," Vint countered, "Perhaps not. He may be just trying to get the cops to look in another direction."

"Was the questioning tough?"

"Nah. Boring mostly—I kept nodding off. It really got their goats."

"So—where do we go from here?" Cilla asked.

"You're the detective."

"I'm not talking about the case."

"You mean...us?"

"Yeah. I know we're in the middle of a case and all, but this...*thing* between us is going to get in the way sooner or later. Heck, is *has* gotten in the way."

Vint stepped over to the table and held out

his hands. Cilla reached out and took them, allowing Vint to draw her to her feet. Then, he bent to kiss her, gathering her up in his arms and almost lifting her off her feet. Cilla's arms went around Vint's neck. For a long while they just stood like that, their lips pressed together, breathing heavily. Finally, they broke it off and Vint lowered Cilla onto her feet.

"God help me, but this was all I could think about all during the questioning last night," Vint admitted.

"Well, I guess that answers my question," Cilla said, smiling up at him.

"Cilla, all during the questioning I realized I loved you—very much. When you came to me earlier, with your suspicions about Amy, and the van, I thought I'd lost you forever. It nearly broke my heart."

Cilla's expression grew serious. "Mine too. I was already shaken from finding out you knew Amy. Then, when I heard about the van from Mrs. Danzig, I cried all the way here. Just the thought that you could be the killer turned my heart to ice."

"I guess this is the spot in the movies where I sweep you up in my arms and carry you off to the bedroom."

"I'm not so sure I'd mind," Cilla breathed.

Vint took her hands in his. "But this isn't the movies and I'm just a simple country preacher. So, I'm just going to go upstairs and take a shower—alone. You're worth waiting for and I want to do this right. Besides, we're not exactly on the same page faith-wise."

Cilla answered by standing on tiptoe and pulling Vint into another long kiss. When she broke it off, she surprised him by whispering in his ear, "Then...pray for me. I'm not as strong as you are."

As Vint headed upstairs, he pondered Cilla's whispered words.

ANOTHER BRONSON VICTIM FOUND! PASTOR BROUGHT IN FOR QUESTIONING.

The paper's headline screamed out yet another lurid bit of news.

"This is getting sickening," Vint said in disgust as he read the paper at the breakfast table, "and now, the mob's out on the yard again."

"I'd advise against going out there this time," Cilla, who had spent the night in the guestroom, pointed out, "I already called Susan. She'll be out to try to restore some sort of order."

"She's sure been a brick about all this," Vint said.

"She's the best," Cilla added, "She's a good match for Jim Fournier."

"Fournier? The Altoona coroner?"

"Yep, the very same. She's been seeing him for almost a year."

"That's good. I'm glad to see she has a life

beyond that badge."

Once Susan had dealt with the media crowd camped out in front of the parsonage, Cilla went on her way.

"So, what's on the agenda today?" Vint asked.

"I think I'll swing by the Baumann's to interview them."

"Would it be okay if I came on this one?"

Cilla was about to say no but changed her mind. "So, want to see the sleuth in action?"

"Something like that," Vint said, smiling, "I like looking at you."

Cilla's face colored, in spite of herself. "Ooo-kay then. Let's be off."

"This is quite a setup you have here," Vint said to Cilla, as they rode together in her van.

"Tools of the trade. I told you I was serious about succeeding in this profession."

"You certainly are thorough, I'll give you that."

"I know — it's one of the things you love about me."

"In a way, yes. It's all part of the package named Priscilla Edwina Stephenson."

"Hmmm, you make my name sound good."

"Do I?"

"You have a way with words. And a way without them too."

"If you say so."

"Oh, but I do. And I have first-hand information on it."

Vint and Cilla looked at one another, shared a smile, and passed the rest of the trip in silence.

When they arrived at the Baumann house, Cilla turned to Vint. "Look, on second thought, it might be better if you stayed in the van. After all, you're a suspect. The Baumanns would probably clam up with you there."

"You have a point. Okay, I'll wait here."

Cilla reached back and took what looked like a camera flash reflector, connected to a set of earphones, from a box behind the passenger seat. She plugged the unit into a power strip mounted under the dash. "Here. Aim this at the front window and you'll be able to hear every word."

"Wow, this gives the word privacy a whole new meaning."

"Yeah — ain't technology grand. Another tool of the trade for surveillance purposes."

"Remind me not to get on your bad side," Vint said, looking down at the equipment in his lap.

"I realize I've come at a bad time," Cilla said to Mr. and Mrs. Baumann across the coffee table. On it was a cup of coffee and her recorder. "Please forgive any painful questions. I'll try to be brief."

"Thank you for your sensitivity," Mrs. Baumann said.

"It's the least I could do. Let's begin, shall we? Jennifer was seeing Stuart Loeb. What did you think of him?"

"I thought he was a jerk," Mr. Baumann answered, "Oh, he was nice enough to us, but he seemed too full of himself—too smarmy."

"What's your impression of Reverend Montrose?"

"He's a nice young man," Mrs. Baumann said, "I wish Jennifer had been seeing him instead of that Loeb fellow."

"And you, Mr. Baumann?"

"He seemed okay to me. A good preacher too. My personal opinion is he's innocent."

"Did Jennifer show any interest in him?" Cilla asked.

"She did mention that she would like to go out with him," Mrs. Baumann answered.

"But no dates you can remember?"

"No. Not that I recall."

"Getting back to Loeb, did you notice any evidence that he was abusive to Jennifer?"

"I heard her crying in her room a time or two," Mrs. Baumann offered, "but she didn't appear to have bruises or anything. He didn't seem to make her happy at all."

"Kathy over at the diner mentioned that Jennifer was friendly to Helen's son Harry. Did he seem to pay any undue attention to her?"

"Who? Harry?" Mr. Baumann asked, "No, he's harmless. The only time he had anything to do with Jennifer, was when he would talk to her in the diner. He adored her—probably because she was nice to him."

"Thank you. Is there anyone else you can think of who had anything to do with Jennifer in the past few days?"

Mrs. Baumann spoke up. "Come to think of it, we were at Maggie's, having our Thursday supper there. Jennifer had a bouquet she wanted to give to Harry. She was at the counter giving it to him, when that Jenks man came up to her and made a point of saying hello. He interrupted Harry, who was agitated by it."

"Then what happened?"

"Jenks left and Jennifer finished up with Harry. When she came back to the table, she was visibly upset but, when I asked her about it, she passed it off as nothing. I was concerned—I never did like that Jenks fellow—but didn't want to press Jennifer over it."

"I see. Well, thank you both for your time," Cilla said, offering her card, "May I talk with you again, should the need arise?"

"Certainly, Mrs. Baumann said.

"That was interesting there at the end," Vint said to Cilla when she entered the van.

"Yeah, a little," Cilla replied, lost in thought,

"which reminds me." Cilla flipped open her cellphone and speed-dialed a call. "Hi, Susan, I wonder if you could do something for me. I need you to check out Jenks for me. I know, but I want you to dig deeper, see what you come up with. Yes, that'll be fine."

"Why are you checking out Jenks?" Vint asked, "He a suspect?"

"Like I said, everyone's a suspect—until he or she isn't."

CHAPTER 9:
THE THICK PLOTTENS

When Vint opened the door of the parsonage, Cilla stood there, wearing khaki shorts, a blue tee shirt, and a khaki bush jacket. Her feet were clad in clunky trail boots. Her black hair was pulled back in a loose ponytail and she wore a black baseball cap, with S.W.A.T. embroidered in yellow across the crown.

"You look like a cop on safari," Vint quipped.

"You were expecting heels and a sheath dress?" Cilla retorted, "I'm dressed appropriately for where we're going. *You* certainly look comfortable enough."

Vint looked down at his cotton, short-sleeved plaid shirt, jeans, and sneakers. "Yeah. Well, I...."

"We'd better be going," Cilla said, brushing past him, effectively ending any further debate.

They pulled up to the barn in Vint's car. An anonymous phone call had specified this meeting place.

"Okay." Cilla said, pushing her door open.

"Looks like we got here first. Let's check out

the barn. Stay alert."

"Yes *sir*!" Vint said, earning a withering look from Cilla.

"This isn't a game. We're investigating a *murder*, in case you forgot. Not staying alert could get us killed."

"Sorry."

They entered the decrepit barn through the partly open, sagging, front door. Sunlight streamed in through numerous holes in the roof and shone off myriads of floating dust motes. They had gotten about halfway through, when a noise in the rafters startled them. Cilla whirled, her right arm going behind her. By the time she had turned, her two arms in the classic weaver stance, her small hands contained the largest revolver Vint had ever seen. The noise turned out to be a couple of pigeons. It was a scene right out of an action flick.

"Jeez!" Vint exclaimed, "You're packing a...a *cannon*!"

Cilla shot Vint a withering stare. "And why not? We're out here in the sticks, for a meeting with some mysterious caller, and you don't think we could possibly encounter danger?"

"It was only a bird."

"And if it wasn't?"

"Okay, point taken. But I think you can put the heat away for now."

Cilla de-cocked the gun and tucked it back in the waistband of her skirt, in the small of her back, where she had a holster for it.

"Now I see why the bush jacket. I figured it was too hot for it."

"I may not have been a Boy Scout, but I always try to be prepared," Cilla said.

"I suppose you can't be to heavily armed for the odd pige...." Vint never finished his witticism because he dropped from sight as if through a trap door. In fact, he *did* drop through a trap door in the floor of the old barn.

"Vint!" Cilla yelled, running to the hole in the dusty floor. She looked down into the hole and saw Vint struggling to his feet in the dirt at the bottom of the eight-foot deep hole.

"Thank God!" Cilla exclaimed in relief, as Vint looked up at her. She had imagined he would be lying in a pool of blood impaled on a myriad of pungi-stakes. She saw Vint's eyes widen, and was about to question him about it, when a sharp blow to the back of her head made everything go black.

Vint sat at the interview table, brooding under the hooded light over his head. The room he was in looked like the ones he had seen in just about every cop show on TV. The interrogating officers, Lieutenant Frary and Sergeant Dunne, had left for a moment giving Vint a rest from the incessant questions.

After Cilla had been knocked unconscious,

and while he looked helplessly on, a ski-masked figure peered over the rim of the hole and then disappeared. Vint had yelled himself hoarse but despaired of ever getting out of his predicament. He jumped, but the edge of the hole was just too far over his head. The dirt on the sides was loose and crumbly, so climbing out was an exercise in futility.

Finally, long after dark, Vint fell exhausted into a sitting position and slept. He dreamed that he dug out enough dirt from the sides of the hole to pile it up and allow his escape, but awoke to the sounds of sirens and didn't get a chance to try it for real. His release from the hole ended in this interrogation room.

When the police arrived, and had gotten him out of his prison, he asked them how they knew he was in there. They said they had received an anonymous call—and that he was under arrest.

For what seemed like hours and hours, Vint tried to patiently answer the questions fired at him. He tried to explain that he went there with Cilla, following an anonymous tip. He described what had happened to him, but his interrogators weren't convinced by his "story." They knew nothing of any private eye having seen him. In truth, Vint couldn't prove he had seen her. They had driven to the barn in Cilla's van and it wasn't found at the site.

The two officers had responded to another

anonymous tip. The caller had told them he had trapped the killer and the officers had found Vint in the hole. They showed Vint pictures of a young, blonde woman he didn't know and had commenced to badger him for a confession.

Vint's heart sank as he looked at the photo of the poor girl, sank even more when he realized he was being accused of another homicide, and sank to its lowest depth when he thought of Cilla being in the clutches of a monster. Anger rose in him as he considered the fact he had been set up, probably by the killer. But why was he the target of the man's wrath? In spite of his dilemma, Vint worried about Cilla's fate. He prayed she wasn't yet another victim of this monster.

When Cilla came to, she was aware of three things. One, was the complete absence of light. The second was the heavy smell of dankness, as if she were in, or near, moist ground. The third was the fact she was completely naked. She could feel cold cement pressing against her bare back and buttocks. Panic began to bubble to the surface as she imagined herself in the grave. She flung her right arm up and was relieved to encounter, not a coffin lid, but empty air.

Vint sat in his cell, staring at a different wall this time but one that seemed identical to the ones he stared at during other visits. He hung his head in despair, too dispirited to even pray. He hoped against hope that Cilla was still alive.

Cilla had spent the past half-hour exploring her prison. As near as she could determine, she was in a cement room about six feet wide, by nine feet long, by six feet high. The top seemed to be cement as well. There were no doors or windows, only a small, metal grate at one end, made of what she guessed was steel. She could feel cool air coming in, so she was in no danger of suffocating. She wondered if it was night outside and if the vent would allow some light in the daytime. There was no light at all. The enclosure was also completely empty, save for her.

Cilla tried to lift the top but to no avail. It was simply too heavy—and too far above her for her to exert much force. The coolness inside was beginning to get to her and she began to shiver. She tried pacing back and forth to keep warm but kept going off course in the dark and bumping into the sides, scraping herself. So, she tried squatting in the center of the enclosure, hugging her knees for warmth. It helped a little, but her feet were getting numb from the cold cement.

Vint squinted against the bright, early morning sunlight, as he stepped from the police station. For the umteenth time, he had been released for lack of evidence. The police could find nothing to incriminate him. He wondered why, if he were being framed, the killer didn't try to plant some incriminating evidence. Vint suspected that he was being toyed with.

He didn't spend too much time on worrying over his dilemma, however, for he was frantic over the fate of his erstwhile investigator, Cilla. He had no idea where she might have been taken. Vint figured the best place to start would be back at the old barn. He had no illusions that he would find evidence the police had overlooked. What he did hope for though, was that the murderer who was toying with him would leave a new clue as to Cilla's whereabouts.

Cilla had spent the long night in a misery of uncontrollable shivers. She felt like the cold had completely soaked through her naked skin right through to her bones. She tried to move around as much as possible in the cramped space. She stood, she sat, and she lay down, in an attempt to stay awake. She didn't think the temperature, which she guessed was in the mid-fifties, would cause extreme hypothermia just yet, but she wasn't going to be able to stave it off indefinitely.

To take her mind off her misery, Cilla thought of the talks she had had with Vint, especially the one on the porch swing when she had completely broken down. That had set her back a bit. Usually so self-confident, she was surprised at her allowance of so much vulnerability. Yet Vint had been great, holding her and just rocking with her for a long time. She remembered that, in addition to her thoughts about God, she had found being against Vint's chest quite pleasurable. Cilla had rejected that feeling at the time but now that she was in the predicament she was in she allowed herself to explore her feelings toward Vint. But what exactly were those feelings? Did she love him as much as he said he loved her?

When the sun had finally come up, Cilla noticed a faint glow coming from the vent. It grew brighter until it was a steady, if diffused, spot of light that illuminated her prison. She reasoned that a pipe probably extended from the vent and made a turn, thus not allowing light to come in directly. Cilla's spirits leaped at the cessation of total darkness. She took some time to study her surroundings but the light only confirmed what her fingers had told her. She was in what could be described as a cement tank, with only the vent as a means for air to get in. The floor was relatively clean of dirt or debris — or anything that could sustain life. If no one came for her, she would slowly starve, or die of thirst and hypothermia. With that grim thought, she noticed how dry her mouth was.

As if that weren't enough, Cilla felt a familiar urge. It figured. It struck her as ironic. Here she was, facing starvation and she had to defecate. She went to the corner opposite the vent, squatted, and relaxed her bowels. Unlike sitting on a toilet, there was no water to stifle the smell and the strong odor of her own feces assaulted her nostrils. Cilla's eyes filled with tears as she endured this further indignity. She was naked, squatting in the corner of her prison, defecating like an animal in its cage. She wondered how much lower into humiliation she could sink.

When Cilla finished, she moved into the opposite corner and tried to get comfortable. She sat there, thinking and dozing for awhile. But soon, she would start awake—driven awake by shivers and by a nagging fear. Sitting here in this cement-lined hole, she realized she was in the same physical condition that all the other victims were found in.

As Cilla's mind drifted, she began to think about God. She remembered how Vint had described his faith and the way he explained God's dealings with mankind. At times their conversation became heated and she had cast her share of barbs in his direction. Yet, he never wavered in his response. For the first time in her life, Cilla had thought of something outside her experience. Vint had described a *personal* deity, one who was actually interested in the affairs of people. Cilla had to admit that it had stopped her cold. She could argue all she wanted to but she couldn't escape what Vint had said. She suddenly realized that it was why she became defensive. At that moment, she wanted to reach out to God—to pray. She decided that it would be best to talk out loud.

"Um, Sir...I really don't know how I should

pray to you, and I know it's only because I'm in trouble, but I just wanted to say I've been thinking about what Vint told me. I also know I haven't ever given you much thought before and I'm sorry about that — I really, truly am. I'm sorry I gave Vint such a hard time when he tried to tell me about you. Please look out for him and help him if he needs it. And, uh, if you don't mind, could you help me out if it's okay? I know I'm lousy at praying and religious stuff, but Vint says you really love us. So...I'm asking as best I know how. Um, thanks Sir...God, I mean...amen."

Having prayed her first real prayer, Cilla felt somehow better. She leaned her head back and tried to remember the times in her life when God might have looked out for her. Huddled naked, in the cement corner of what amounted to a tomb, possibly hours away from a gruesome death, Cilla inextricably began to feel release from the hard knot of anger and resentment she had stifled all her life.

Vint stopped at the parsonage and got out the old bird gun he stored in the bedroom closet. He put on his bush jacket and emptied an almost full box of shells into the large right cargo pocket. He loaded five cartridges into the magazine of the pump-action twenty-gauge.

He got into his battered Beetle and headed out to the old barn. On the way there, he sent many fervent prayers up to a God he was beginning to feel was a distant presence at best. He never considered the incongruity of the shotgun propped against the passenger seat.

Despite her best efforts, Cilla had fallen asleep. She was stretched out on the cold cement floor when she was startled awake by the cement-on-cement scrape of the lid of her prison. A thin and growing line of light assaulted her dark-blinded eyes and she squinted against it. She hurried to get up, dismayed at how stiff and sore her joints and muscles were. Her mouth felt like dry cotton. She made it to her feet and stumbled to the opposite corner, where she had collected what she hoped would be a surprise for her captor.

The lid slid half off the top and Cilla had to nearly close her eyes at the sudden infusion of bright light. She blinked and squinted until she could open them a bit. She could see her prison was in another building—a tin-roofed shed she guessed. In another moment, a head and shoulders were framed in the opening. The head was covered in a ski mask. Two arms reached over the edge of the wall, holding a plastic, half-gallon jug of water, and a plastic shopping bag, weighted down with what Cilla figured was food.

Her captor seemed to be waiting for her to take them, so Cilla moved to where they dangled. She raised her arms as if to take the proffered items but instead threw two handfuls of fine cement dust into the eyes that peered through the ski mask. She had laboriously scraped and swept together any dust she could glean until her hands were raw, and had been rewarded with a fair pile of dust for her efforts. Now its lime-based grit was burning the eyes of her captor.

The ski-masked, would-be jailer dropped the jug and bag and let out with an involuntary howl. Cilla was surprised to hear a woman's voice. She launched herself up to the edge, managing to get one arm over the side. She flailed with her feet against the wall and hooked one foot over the edge. She could feel the rough cement scratching against her bare breasts and stomach but she gritted her teeth against the pain and scrabbled to get herself up and over the top. In a few more seconds she was out!

Vint arrived at the old barn. He got out of the Beetle, taking the bird gun with him. Holding it at the ready, he entered. He could see where the hole he had fallen into was now filled in. The ground over it looked undisturbed — tamped and swept clean, no doubt. No wonder the police didn't believe his story. There were myriad footprints all around the dirt floor of the barn — obvious evidence of a thorough search for clues. Vint's despondency at not being able to find Cilla until it was too late returned with a vengeance.

Then, Vint noticed the paper in the middle of the floor, held down with a rock. It had to have been left there recently, since the police had not discovered it. He hurried to where it lay and snatched it up. There was just one hand-printed line on it—JENKS' F&G. Vint knew that it referred to the old feed and grain complex just outside of Bronson. He ran back to the VW and headed there in a spray of dirt and gravel, not wondering for a moment who had left the note.

Cilla fell over the rim of her cement prison into the dust and scrambled to get to her feet. Dirt was caked on the bloody scratches on her bare front. She was naked and sore—but determined that her tormentor was *not* going to put her back in that hole. Rising to a crouch, Cilla could see her captor standing a short way off, clawing at her face, trying to wipe the dust out of her smarting eyes. Heedless of the fact she was totally bare, Cilla ran over to the woman and gave her a vicious kick in the stomach. The woman fell onto her back, uttering a loud "Ooof!" Cilla jumped on her, straddling her and punching her in the face, putting every ounce of her fury into each blow. The woman went limp and fell back. Cilla grabbed her hood and yanked it off. The face that was revealed caused her to gasp. It was a caricature of a woman's face, distorted not from an injury but malformed in the womb. Cilla had little time to ponder over the injustices of nature, however, for a voice behind her caused her blood to run cold.

"Well, well, well. Now ain't this a pretty picture," a man's voice said sarcastically.

Cilla rose and turned to face — Jenks! He wore a flannel shirt, greasy bib overalls, and a pair of work boots popular with farmers. He clutched a large revolver in his grimy paw. Cilla recognized it as hers.

"Y'know, you ain't a half-bad little piece-a-ass, even plump as you are. Nice and busty too. The blood and dirt's a nice touch — turns me on, it does."

Cilla glared at Jenks. If he were trying to goad her, she wouldn't rise to the bait.

"I have no idea how you got out, but you sure made short work outa my daughter. Where'd you learn to dish it out like that? Good as any man, you were." The man chuckled at what he considered his sharp wit.

Cilla continued to glare at him.

"Come with me into the store now," he said, waving the revolver in that direction, "Can't have anyone seein' you out here like this." Another chuckle. "I got a nice set of manacles inside for you. Once I get 'em on ya, I can take my time cleaning you up. Then we can have some fun."
Cilla looked over her shoulder. The woman she attacked still lay inert in the dust. It gave Cilla a sense of satisfaction.

"C'mon, move!" Jenks yelled, waving the pistol. "Get up to the store!"

Cilla began walking toward a dilapidated old

storefront with a big sign that said JENKS' FEED AND GRAIN over the front door. Her mind worked in a fever pitch to figure a way out of her plight. *God, please help me!* She prayed in her mind.

Just then, she heard the clatter of a VW Beetle coming in from the main road a quarter of a mile away. Vint! She looked and saw him coming up the dirt road at high speed, dust boiling up all around the small car.

"C'mon, get inside, NOW!" Jenks yelled, looking nervously at the oncoming car, "Or do I gotta shoot ya?"

Cilla walked as slowly as she could past where Jenks was standing, inching imperceptibly closer to him. She watched him out of the corner of her eye. *God, give me the strength and skill I need!* she prayed inwardly. In the heat of the moment she never realized that she was asking for strength outside of herself for probably the first time in her young life.

Just then, she saw the opening she needed. Jenks looked over his shoulder again and Cilla flung herself at him, knocking him off his feet. She struggled with the stunned man, managing to get her hands on the pistol, but he was just too strong for her to wrest it out of his grip. They rolled around in a weirdly erotic embrace, as Cilla fought to prevent Jenks from overpowering her. He managed to roll on top of her. Cilla's strength was dwindling fast. Little by little, she could feel she was losing the uneven contest. When she was almost exhausted, a loud report caused Jenks' struggles to cease. He looked over his shoulder. Cilla wasted no time wresting the revolver from his grip.

"That's enough!" Vint yelled, racking another round into the chamber of his shotgun, which was pointed skyward.

"Vint! Look out!" Cilla yelled, but it was too late.

The woman had come to and ran toward Vint, tackling him. They wrestled in the dust for the shotgun. Meanwhile, Jenks recovered his wits enough to snatch the gun from Cilla's hand, slapping her across the face with the barrel. Cilla felt the blow crack something and saw lights go on inside her skull in a blinding burst of pain. She fell onto her back. Jenks turned and drew a bead on Vint, unable to shoot because he and the woman were rolling around in the dust. Finally, Vint overpowered her, snatched the shotgun away, and jumped to his feet.

"Stop right there Reverend," Jenks yelled, "Can't have you shootin' my kin now. Drop that scattergun!" Vint dropped the shotgun and involuntarily raised both hands. "My girl gave you a real tussle, didn't she? Almost as strong as a man. Not much to look at though. Things were different, you two'd make a good match. Makes me feel bad about havin' ta shoot ya."

"So, you're the one who killed all those

women," Vint said, as he dropped the shotgun in the dust, trying to buy some time. Out of the corner of his eye, he saw the woman get up and walk his way to retrieve the shotgun.

"Couldn't let 'em live once my girl here got done playin' with 'em," Jenks said, as though he were mentioning the price of corn.

"Your girl?" Vint asked, incredulous, "You mean—*she* was the rapist?"

The woman stopped and looked at her father. The look he returned was almost tender.

"When you're born lookin' like her, things goin' on behind that face get screwed up too, I guess. Since boys was out of the question, she turned her affection toward women. Guess it was 'cuz a the beauty she never had. So, I helped her get 'em."

"You mean to tell me you did all this to help your daughter?" Vint asked, dumbfounded.

"She's kin after all," Jenks said, smiling in his daughter's direction. Her ravaged face distorted into something resembling a smile. "She ain't much to look at but she's all I got. Her mother died a-bornin' her. Raised her myself from a newborn. Didn't have the heart to end her life—even ugly as she was. Been a good daughter to me. Strong as a ox—a real hard worker. Only fittin' I do what I kin for her."

"Oh, my dear Lo...."

Vint had only begun his answer, when two things happened simultaneously. First, the woman bent to retrieve the shotgun and, second, Cilla piled into Jenks in a flying tackle.

"Vint—the shotgun!" Cilla screamed, as she landed on top of the surprised man, both of her hands on the revolver.

Vint brought up his knee and caught the daughter in the face. She grunted and fell away. Vint snatched the shotgun out of the dust. He saw that Jenks had gotten the upper hand in his contest with Cilla. He had the revolver and had risen to one knee. He brought the gun around to shoot Cilla, but a loud report caused him to fly sideways and land in a heap, one side of his body a bloody mess. Vint had shot him from less than fifteen feet away.

The daughter let out with a blood-curdling scream and tackled Vint. They went down in a tangle of arms and legs. In seconds, the daughter somersaulted away from Vint, the shotgun in her hands. She ended up on her feet, shotgun at the ready. Vint turned to face the inevitable. The woman raised the shotgun...

...And flew back—a deafening explosion punctuating the moment. She hit the ground like a sack of potatoes, a large, wet stain coloring the front of her black sweatshirt. Vint turned and saw Cilla, gripping the .357 Magnum in a classic two-handed weaver stance, feet apart, in a slight crouch. The only thing that made the scene look jarringly out of place was the fact that Cilla was dirty, bloody—and stark naked.

Vint looked at Cilla's small face where she sat next to him on the fender of his car. The right side of it was caked with blood, the swelling nearly shutting her eye. Where there was no blood, a layer of grime covered it. In spite of that, Cilla was smiling.

"I know it's probably the adrenaline talking, but I'm *sooo* psyched!"

"Adrenaline or not, you sound far too chipper," Vint said, as he snapped his cell phone shut after a call to the police.

"And why not?" Cilla countered, "After everything that happened, all the right people are still standing."

Vint unbuttoned his shirt and shrugged out of it. "Here, put this on. Let's not give the police any more of a shock. Your face'll be enough."

Cilla looked down at the front of her dirt and blood-caked body. "Yeah, I guess I don't look too fetching at the moment. But, the important part is — we're alive — and that's what counts."

"At the cost of two lives," Vint said sadly.

"Hey! What would you have preferred?" Cilla said, her tone angry, "They were killers, Vint — sick, twisted killers. It could just as easily have been us lying there in the dust. Think about that."

Vint looked at Cilla, smarting from her rebuke. "Perhaps you consider it all in a day's work — and believe me, I'm happy we're alive — but two people are dead at our hands."

"Don't go all weak-sister on me, Vint. We both did what we had to do."

"Is that what you think of me—as weak?"

Cilla looked into Vint's eyes, seeing the hurt there. She realized what had taken place was so far out of Vint's experience it was inconceivable to him. He was a man of faith, trained to try to bring out the good in people—not prepared to take out deviants. For that matter, neither was she. But, she had her hard core of anger to pull her through. As difficult as it might be to kill another human being, she harbored no regrets for doing what had to be done. And, there was no doubt in her mind she would do it again, should the need arise.

Cilla raised her hand and laid it on Vint's cheek. "Look, Sweetie, we did what we did to save one another. Besides, I asked God for help and he answered me by sending you at the exact moment I needed you."

Vint surprised Cilla by smiling. "*Sweetie?* I can't believe you just called me Sweetie. And you *prayed?*"

Cilla looked up into Vint's eyes, pleased to see the hurt gone. "While I was down in that cement coffin over there, I had time to do a lot of thinking. Let me tell you, being stark naked in the dark, having to defecate in a corner, is…shall we say, humbling. I thought about what you had told me and I prayed that God would look after you and help me too. I guess he answered."

Vint returned Cilla's gaze. Her earnestness, coupled with the sorry condition of her poor face, combined to get through all his defenses.

Cilla, not hearing a response from Vint, looked up. "What? Why are you looking at me like that?"

"Does this mean you decided to trust God?"

"I guess it does at that," Cilla answered, "So?"

"Enough to trust him as your savior?"

"Well, he did save me, after all," Cilla answered.

"Would you like to pray with me right now?"

"You mean—*now*, now? But...I'm a mess. And I'm wearing nothing but your shirt for Pete's sake!"

"Did the fact that you were naked down in that hole stop you from praying? Do you think God cares what you're wearing?"

"Well, I guess not. But I don't know how to pray right—I'm no good at religious stuff. And what about you? A minute ago, you were beating yourself up for doing what you had to do."

"Tell you what. I'll help you—and you can help me. Deal?"

"Okay."

The two of them fell silent and Cilla moved up against Vint, enjoying being with him even in circumstances like this. She pondered what had transpired. She had come to Bronson to help her career as a new private detective. What she had found nearly cost her her life. But, she had also found a handsome young minister and a new personal faith. She remembered the old bromide, "God works in mysterious ways his wonders to perform." In the distance, the warble of police sirens intruded on Cilla's reverie. She hoped it'd be awhile before they got to them.

CHAPTER 10:
ENDGAME

Vint and Cilla stood on the back loading dock of the Bronson hospital, where the ambulance had taken them both after the incident at Jenks' place. They had been thoroughly examined and given a clean bill of health. Cilla had suffered the most injuries, including exposure. Earlier, Susan Kroeger went to the parsonage, where she had picked up some fresh clothes for Vint and Cilla. Now, she pulled up to dock and hopped out of the Explorer. She picked them up there due to the reporters camped out at the front entrance.

"Whoooeee!" Susan said when she got a good look at Cilla's face, "You look like you came out second best in a kissing contest with a black bear."

"Is that one of those pithy country sayings?" Cilla said, smiling—then wincing from the pain it caused.

"Something like that. You going to be okay?"

"Nothing a few weeks of healing can't cure. I

still shudder when I think of how close I came to becoming a candidate for Jim Fournier's autopsy table."

"But you didn't. And — not only that — you and Vint solved what's stacking up to be a real doozy of a murder case — not that there's much of a case with both culprits dead. Besides saving the county a lot of money, you two are going to be celebrities — and the Bronson Police Department is going to look like Mayberry County's finest."

"You think so?" Cilla asked as she and Vint got into the back of the Explorer and Susan drove off.

"I know so. My Dad's the Chief of police, don't forget. He's been beside himself the last couple of days. No one'll go near him for fear of being shot."

"No offense, but this case was a bit out of the Bronson Police Department's league."

"And you sashay into town and break the case wide open all by your lonesome — you and Vint. You two sure have given the Bronson Police Department something to think about. I wouldn't be visiting the station any time too soon, if I were you. Don's not too happy of late either."

"Yeah, I'm a regular whiz kid. My breaking the case wide open nearly cost me my life," Cilla said wistfully.

"Have you got anything on the Jenks pair?" Vint asked, interrupting the downward spiral of the previous dialogue.

"Oh yeah," Susan said, nodding, "Lester Jenks and his daughter were a real pair. It seems she was his sister Leslie's baby. Leslie died in childbirth and Lester brought her up. Want to take a guess as to who the father was?"

"Oh no...Jenks *himself?*" Vint asked.

"You got it in one. Lester kept his deformed daughter out of sight all these years. After Leslie's death, when she wasn't around to keep his peculiar appetites under control, Lester's predilections finally got out of hand and he turned to murder. You won't believe what we found, though."

"What?" Cilla and Vint asked in unison.

"The daughter Luann was doing the dirty work. We found a bunch of sex toys, including a dildo harness, that Luann evidently used to rape the women — a real twisted sister. It seems Lester got his jollies strangling them. The whole thing turns my stomach."

"Oh my dear Lord," Vint exclaimed.

Susan arrived at the parsonage and pulled to the curb. "Here you go — part of the service. Cilla, you asked me to investigate Jenks' background just before he abducted you. Why?"

"To tell you the truth, I was just trying to cover all the bases. Plus, I had a nagging suspicion about him from the morning I stopped by to talk with him."

"Well, your instincts were right on target," Susan observed, "Look, you two did this town a real service, and I, for one, don't mind that the department came up short. It'll make us do our homework from now on. Maybe Dad'll start listening to me more now about modernizing. You both have my deepest thanks."

"Thank you Susan," Cilla said.

"Susie," Susan said, "My friends call me Susie." With that, she stepped forward and hugged Cilla.

After Cilla and Susan hugged, Vint took Susan's hand.

"Thanks for all you've done—for me and for Cilla. She's told me how much you helped her."

"I'm glad I did. Well, I have to get back and face the music. When do you want me to take you to see Jim?"

"Would tomorrow morning be okay?"

"Sure—tomorrow morning it is. I'll swing by around eight if that isn't too early."

"No, that's fine. See you tomorrow at eight."

"Okay then. 'Bye, folks," Susan said, as she climbed into the Explorer and pulled away.

Vint took Cilla's elbow and guided her up the walk to the house. She moved like an eighty-year-old. When they got to the porch, Cilla spoke.

"I'd like to just sit out here and enjoy the afternoon air, if you don't mind."

"Not at all," Vint said, "I'll order a pizza and we can sit out here and enjoy it."

"Sounds like a dream," Cilla replied

gratefully.

While the two of them waited for the pizza, Vint asked Cilla a question. "So, what will you do from here on?"

"I guess my reputation has been made," Cilla mused, "I can pick and choose my cases. Y'know, I couldn't have done any of what I did without you. Besides being a good minister, you're one heck of a good detective. You've got great instincts."

"How do you know?"

"Know? Well, just look how you...."

"Not the detective part—about me being a good minister."

"Well, you got through to me didn't you?"

"Not me. It was the Holy Spirit."

"Yes, but who did the talking?"

"As God led me," Vint said, hoping he didn't sound falsely humble. At that moment, he realized just how much he loved Cilla. This vibrant, cocky bundle of energy had come into his life at its lowest point and rescued him from a curse. Then God had *doubly* blessed him with the joy of seeing her come to faith. He realized he couldn't let her go out of his life—not after almost losing her.

"Vint?"

Vint looked at Cilla. "What?"

"Wow, you sure got introspective all of a sudden," Cilla joked.

"I was thinking about you—about us," Vint

answered, looking into Cilla's eyes.

"And...?"

"About how much I love you."

For once, Cilla was speechless. Vint decided to let actions speak louder than words and leaned in to gently lay his lips on Cilla's. She winced at first, but soon returned Vint's kiss with a fervor that matched his.

Vint walked out to the kitchen at 3AM, to find Cilla sitting at the kitchen table with a cup of instant coffee.

"I thought I heard something," he said, causing Cilla, who was deep in thought, to jump. "Sorry, I thought you knew I was here."

"Don't be. I was lost in thought."

"Oh? The case is solved. What's there to think about?"

"How did you know where to find me?"

"Huh? What do you mean?"

" Well, in all the confusion and excitement, I never considered it. So, how *did* you find me?"

"I found a note in the barn where I fell in the hole."

"A note?"

"Yeah, it had *Jenks' F&G* printed on it. I headed right out there as soon as I read...oh Lord, *who* put the note there?"

"Precisely. If you recall, someone put my lights out, leaving you in the hole. Besides, I had no idea where I was."

"Then, who wrote the note and left it where I would find it? And, how did they know I'd go there?"

"It's not too much of a stretch for whoever it was to figure you'd want to go to the place where you were ambushed. But, why leave the note? Beyond that, why be secretive about it? Wait! I just thought of something else. Who let the cops know you were in the hole?"

"Wow, no wonder you're awake at three in the morning. Hey! Do you suppose the person who left the note was the same person who called the police?"

"Shall I make a cup of coffee for you too?" Cilla said, smiling.

Later that morning, Cilla and Vint stood on the Smithfield's front porch. Mrs. Smithfield was the one to answer the door. She pulled it open and gave them her best non-communicative look.

"Is your husband at home?" Cilla asked.

The woman looked at them without speaking for so long, Cilla fully expected her to slam the door in their faces. "Yes, but he's in the fields."

"Do you have a way to reach him?" Vint asked, impatience in his voice.

Mrs. Smithfield dropped her gaze then met his eyes again. "We have cellphones."

"Could you call him, please?" Cilla asked, "We need to speak to you both." To Cilla's surprise, the woman complied without dissembling.

Before driving over to the Smithfield's farm, Cilla and Vint had pulled an all-nighter. Each nursing cups of coffee, they discussed who might have left the mysterious note and called the police.

"I think it was someone either you or I already know, or have met," Cilla surmised.

"What makes you say that?" Vint asked.

"Simple logic. In my admittedly limited experience, things come out of the blue only in mystery novels. What the average person fails to realize is that people involved in crimes are more connected with one another than may be evident. Bronson is a small town. That fact narrows the odds considerably."

For hours, the two pored over the possibilities. Finally, Cilla made up her mind.

"I think we need to pay a visit to the Smithfields," she said definitively.

"The Smithfields? Why them? You only questioned them about the location of one of the bodies."

"I'm still playing a hunch here, but we need to talk with their daughter."

"Their daughter? Why? She's at college — right?"

"Perhaps."

Cilla and Vint were seated opposite the Smithfields like the ranks of two opposing armies.

The Smithfields were as communicative as ever, which meant the room was eerily quiet.

"Is your daughter here?" Cilla asked, out of the blue. Vint snapped his head to look at Cilla, surprised by her verbal bombshell.

Mrs. Smithfield looked at her husband for a long time. Finally, they turned to look back at Cilla and Vint.

"Yes," Mrs. Smithfield said in a small voice, "She's up in her room."

"She was here when I first questioned you, wasn't she?" Cilla continued, unruffled by the revelation.

"Yes," Mrs. Smithfield said, dropping her gaze to her folded hands.

"Why did you lie to me, ma'am?"

Vint expected Mr. Smithfield to interrupt, but he remained passively quiet, content to let his wife do the talking.

"I didn't want to involve her in this."

"Why?"

A tear leaked from Mrs. Smithfield's right eye and traced its way down her cheek. "She'd been seeing that Loeb boy. I never liked him. Always seemed to be up to no good and so cock-sure of himself."

"I've questioned him and I agree with you there, but why did you feel your daughter needed to be protected?"

Mrs. Smithfield gave Cilla a pleading look. "He dated that Baumann girl, you know—the one who was murdered. I was afraid...."

"Afraid he might be the killer I was looking for?" Mrs. Smithfield nodded. "If that were true, didn't you think she'd be in danger from him?"

"She'd stopped seeing him months ago. I didn't want her implicated in anything."

"That's all well and good, but did it occur to you that, by not telling me what you knew, you might have been preventing us from capturing the killer?"

Again, Mrs. Smithfield nodded.

Cilla sighed heavily and rubbed her eyes. "Could you ask her to join us?"

Mrs. Smithfield got up and left, returning a couple of minutes later with her daughter. She looked like a younger, prettier version of her mother.

"This is Serena," Mrs. Smithfield stated by way of an introduction.

Cilla got up and stuck out her hand. "Hello, Serena."

Serena took her hand, shook it, and said "Hi," almost inaudibly. Then, she took a seat next to her mother.

"Serena, were you the one who called the police and left the note?" Cilla asked. Serena nodded, then broke down completely, burying her face in her mother's bosom. "Why did you do that? If you knew what was going on, why not just tip off the police to the killer?"

Serena sat up and took a tissue her mother

offered. She blew her nose and mopped her eyes. "I thought Stuart might be the killer, but I wasn't sure," she said in a tiny voice, "I didn't want him to think it was me who told on him. He can be a brutal man when he's angry. It's why I broke up with him. I thought he'd just show up and kill me."

"But you must have known the police thought that Vint was the killer. Why let them continue to go after the wrong man? And, why let a killer possibly kill again?"

Serena started crying again. "I wasn't thinking straight—I was *so* scared!" she blurted, "I guess I'm just a coward."

Cilla looked up and turned her gaze on Mr. Smithfield. "Look at my face, Mr. Smithfield. The killer did this to me. He'd have killed me too, if Vint hadn't intervened. If you had only called the police with what you knew, perhaps none of this would have happened." Having said her piece, Cilla stood. "Come on Vint—let's go home." The two of them headed for the door, but were stopped by Mrs. Smithfield's voice.

"What will happen to Serena now?" she asked.

Cilla turned to look at her. "Nothing much. The police may want to talk with her, but the killers are dead and the case is closed."

"What the heck was that all about?" Vint asked on the way to the car.

"What do you mean?" Cilla asked.

"Come *on*—you know as well as I do that the note had Jenks' granary on it. She said she thought it was Loeb. Why let her off the hook like that?"

"I have my reasons."

"Oh, so now you get all mysterious. Think you could share your thoughts with the guy who saved your life?"

"To tell you the truth, I'm not sure what my thoughts are at this point."

"What?"

"I was fishing in there. I only had a suspicion that Serena was our mystery tipper. She also knew that I knew she was lying. After all, she wrote the note."

"But still, why let her off the hook?"

"I don't know...perhaps to spare her parents."

"Then...what now?"

"We wait and see."

CHAPTER 11:
SUDDEN DEATH OVERTIME

Though it was only 9PM, Cilla and Vint were fast asleep in their beds. The lack of sleep the day before, and the activities of the previous day had taken their toll. Cilla had been sleeping fitfully. Every time she hit REM sleep, she began to dream, and her dreams invariably led her back to that cement hole. Suddenly, she came awake and sat bolt upright. She looked around the darkened room, her ears pricked for the slightest sound.

Nothing.

Her heart nearly stopped when a shadow stepped from out of a dark corner.

"You're a light sleeper, I'll give you that," a man's voice said, "Should have been out for the count, considering the past couple of days."

Cilla recognized the voice but couldn't place it.

"Either you're incredibly lucky, or you're the best detective since Sherlock Holmes. I'm still trying to figure how you knew to ask 'Rena about the note."

"This is a small town," Cilla said, impressed

by how steady her voice was, "There weren't too many avenues to go down." The man stepped forward and, because of the small amount of light coming through the window, Cilla could see enough of his face to match it with the voice. "If it's any consolation, Stuart, I wasn't certain you were involved. Now, it makes sense."

"Oh? What do you mean?"

Loeb moved his right arm and Cilla could see the dull glint of a knife blade. Her flesh crawled at the thought of its point piercing her skin.

"I knew Serena was seeing you. She said she had broken up with you, but she lied before. You were working with Jenks, weren't you?"

"It was a sweet deal. His mutant kid did her twisted thing and I killed them. Jenks was only protecting his kid. Sick pair, they were."

"Where does Serena fit in? That's the only thing that has me baffled."

"We weren't sleeping together. Sex don't do it for me. The killing does. She was getting it on with Jenks."

"*Jenks?* Serena was sleeping with *him?*"

"Sleeping wasn't the way to describe it. Those two were into the kinky stuff. Guess Serena got the urges from all the times her old man did her."

"Ah, she was molested by her father. I had my suspicions about that. So, something in Jenks resonated in her twisted self-image. Jenks was a substitute for dear old Dad."

"You're smart. Too smart for your own good."

"You're going to kill me?"

"What do you think?"

"But...they have their man. Why didn't you just hold your peace? You'll only open the case again. They'll find you."

"I don't plan on hanging around."

"You running off with Serena?"

"Hell, no. I'll have to do her next. Too twisted for me."

Loeb ended his dialogue by lunging at Cilla.

Cilla, however, was quicker. While she had engaged Loeb in conversation, relying on the fact he would brag about his deeds, she had slowly slipped her hand under her pillow. She whipped out her trusty .357 magnum, swung it in front of her, and pulled the trigger. The explosion of the powerful gun rocked the room, temporarily deafening her. The light from the flame of the discharge lit up the room like a flashbulb, etching the picture of Loeb's body flying back in stop-motion into her memory.

The knife flew from Loeb's grasp and he hit the floor with a thud that shook the house. A few seconds later, Vint barged into the room. He snapped on the overhead light, saw Loeb on the floor and, with panic etched on his face, looked over at Cilla.

"You've got to get better locks," she said, her ears ringing, noting that the barrel of the gun was oscillating from the shaking of her hands. She dropped it on the coverlet. Long-suppressed sobs and tears bubbled up and Cilla dropped her face into her hands.

"I'm wondering if this town's going to survive all this," Susan Kroeger said, shaking her head sadly. She was sitting on the sofa in Vint's living room, daubing a vitamin E solution onto Cilla's scrapes.

Cilla sat under her ministrations wearing just panties. She held a towel in front of her. "Most people make the mistake that life in the country is all scenery, farms, and Saturday night at the square dance," Cilla observed, "They think all the weirdness is in the cities. But, it isn't like that. Don't feel too bad. The really bad stuff's been purged."

"Yeah, thanks to you. This town owes you debts that can't be repaid."

Just then, Vint entered the room, carrying a tray with sandwiches and cold drinks on it.

"Uh, should the town's reverend be seeing his boarder like this?" Susan asked, non-plussed.

"I've seen a lot more," Vint quipped, smiling, "Besides, you're here to chaperone."

"Somehow, I don't think I'm as alluring as I should be," Cilla added, "I probably look like a case study in cuts and abrasions."

Susan took a break from her medical duties and the three tucked into the food and drink, eating off lap trays.

"What will happen to the Smithfields?" Vint asked around a mouthful of food.

"The daughter will be spending a lot of time in the custody of the State. The father will be prosecuted for child abuse. Mommy Dearest will be spending some time in the same institution as her daughter."

"My God — to think all that was going on in a little town like Bronson," Vint said, shaking his head.

"One of the things that being in law enforcement does for you, is it takes away any illusions about the better angels of our human nature," Susan said.

"Ouch! That sounded so...so world-weary," Vint countered, "How old did you say you were?"

"Let's say I have a different perspective of the human condition. Perhaps if more folks attended your chapel, things would have turned out differently."

After that observation, the remainder of lunch passed in silence. When they had eaten — and Susan had finished doctoring Cilla — Vint stood on the front porch with her to say goodbye.

"Thanks for all you've done, Sue. I'm sure Cilla would say the same."

"Are you kidding? This town had a festering sore at its center and you two lanced it. Hopefully, Bronson can return to something more like normal now." Susan looked up and locked eyes with Vint. "You going to stick around?"

Vint shook his head. "It doesn't seem likely. The social contract between this town and me has taken a big hit. I don't see how I could be effective in my role as minister."

"Too bad," Susan said, sadness tingeing her voice, "You're a good man, Reverend Montrose." Having said her piece, Susan stood on tiptoe and kissed Vint on the cheek. Then, she turned and hurried to her Explorer.

Vint thought he saw the glint of a tear in her eye. "Susan!" he called after her. She stopped and turned to look at him, a question mark on her face. "You settle down with that beau of yours and raise some kids. Life's too short to be waiting around."

Susan merely smiled, her features softening. "I'm on it," she said, winking, and got into her SUV, flipping Vint a casual wave. She started it and sped off in the manner of police the world around.

CHAPTER 12:
TAKING A FORK IN THE ROAD

Cilla lay in the hammock in the parsonage's backyard, catching some warm sunshine. It felt so good on her abused skin! The scabs on her scrapes were peeling off and that left stark white blotches on her normally olive skin.

Since the rural location of the backyard afforded privacy, Cilla doffed her blouse and enjoyed the feel of the sun on her bare skin. She gave not a thought to Vint coming out and seeing her. All kidding aside, he had indeed seen a lot more. Even considering her newfound faith, her showing some of the more intimate portions of her anatomy seemed trivial after all that had occurred.

"Hey Cilla!" Vint called, "I'm coming out, so cover up!

Cilla reluctantly flipped her towel over her bosom. "Okay, but there's not much to see anyway."

"Says you," Vint said, already next to the hammock. He hadn't waited long.

"Now…take you. Were I to see your studly body shirtless, it might be a different story."

"You don't say," Vint quipped, taking a seat in one of the lawn chairs, "But didn't you already?"

"You were wearing a tee shirt. As good as you look in one, it doesn't count."

"Guess I'm going to have to keep my shirt on — don't want you losing control."

The two laughed, then lapsed into a serious silence.

"Where are we going?" Vint asked, giving voice to the unspoken thought shared between them.

"Well, *I'm* going to go back to Philly. I live there, you know."

"Cilla…stop!"

Cilla was brought up short by the sternness of Vint's command. The sudden tears that sprang into her eyes surprised her. She had become quite emotional of late.

"I don't know, Vint," she said softly, chastened, "I remember you saying you loved me. But, of late, since you rescued naked little me, there seems to be a…some distance between us. It's as if you don't feel you can trust yourself around me anymore."

Vint's head snapped up. He looked at Cilla with a serious look on his face. Then, without a word, he got up, walked over to the hammock, and reached down to lift Cilla into his embrace.

He then lowered his head and kissed her, long and passionately. Cilla responded, by throwing her arms around Vint, uncaring of the fact the towel had fallen away when he lifted her.

A few moments later, Vint and Cilla sat in opposing lawn chairs, their knees touching. Cilla had donned her blouse. The two of them held hands.

"You're right," Vint said softly, "There *has* been some distance between us. All that happened has hit me like a two-by-four to the back of the head. I came to this quiet little town to take my first pastorate, only to find out that Bronson harbored a terrible secret...several terrible secrets. It's enough to shake anyone's faith."

"Vint, you're worrying me."

Vint looked into Cilla's eyes. He could see uncertainty there. "Oh, I'm not saying that I've lost mine. It's just that I'm wondering what *I'm* doing here. After all that's happened, I doubt I could run a church as if all of it never took place. Look. I have a proposition for you."

"Oh?" Cilla said, her brows knitted in concern.

"What do you say I take the course you did and we *both* work as detectives?"

"Are you serious?"

"As a judge. As far as I'm concerned, my life in Bronson is over. There's nothing for me here anymore. Besides, you're not cut out to be a minister's wife."

Cilla's expression turned to incredulousness. "Why Reverend Montrose, are you proposing to me?"

"Good deduction, Holmes. Yes, I'm asking you to be my wife. Will you marry me?"

Cilla was so surprised, she temporarily lost her ability for the quick retort. She looked at Vint, who had a small smile on his lips, studying his face. "At least you have it right. You didn't say Watson."

"Is that a yes?"

Cilla dropped her eyes, "Yes," she said softly but firmly, "But I feel so utterly unprepared to be someone's wife."

"It doesn't have to be a big wedding," Vint said, "I could contact my home office and arrange for a minister to come out here. We could use this church, invite Susan and Jim Fournier, and anyone else who would come. What do you say — you're not afraid to take a chance on an ex-pastor are you?"

"So, you're saying we could be a husband and wife detective duo like Nick and Nora North in the *Thin Man* movies?" Cilla quipped, reverting to her comic demeanor.

"I think that's Nick and Nora *Charles*."

"That's what I said."

"No, you said *North*."

"I did? Well, I meant *Charles*."

"Then it's settled?" Vint said, getting back on point, "We get married here?"

Cilla nodded. "You've seen me naked, after all. I guess marriage ought to be the next step."

Vint stood, causing Cilla to jump.

"What?" she said, standing as well.

"You're so flip all the time, I hardly know when you're serious. Was I hearing things, or did you just agree to marry me?"

"How about this?" Cilla stood, threw her arms up around Vint's neck, and pulled him into a long, passionate kiss.

As Vint savored the taste of Cilla's lips, he decided he heard right after all.

Coming soon from

another exciting Cilla Stephenson mystery!

SEASON OF THE VIGILANTE
[A Cilla Stephenson and Vint Montrose Mystery]

CHAPTER 1: MISSION READY

The man stuffed the black duffel with equipment—one hundred feet of climbers' line with D-rings and belaying ring; a pair of wearable night vision goggles; a nine-millimeter Beretta; a silencer for the nine-mil; four extra magazines of ammo; two black balaclavas; a spare pair of black climbers' gloves; a folding, three-inch knife; and a dozen disposable handcuffs. It was obvious he wasn't going camping. In short, he was a man on a mission.

When he had finished, he carried the duffel to his vehicle. It was an old, dull black, nondescript Taurus sedan with limo-dark windows—a car no one would give a second look. He opened the trunk and put the duffel inside.

The man closed the trunk, walked to the driver's door, opened it, and got in. On the seat to his right sat an airline-style carry-on bag. The bag contained a thermos of coffee, sandwiches, a couple of pieces of fruit, and two twenty-ounce bottles of spring water. On the seat next to the bag lay a notepad. The pad contained a list of names. The man opened the pad, selected the names he wanted and placed it next to him on the seat.

The man sighed and rubbed his eyes. Months of planning had culminated in his sitting in this very car. All the pieces had been assembled.

Information had been painstakingly gathered. His plans had been made. Now he was going to put the wheels in motion. After tonight, there would be no turning back—no turning back because he would have taken the first, irrevocable step.

Early on he had had doubts. But now he had gotten past them. He was going to do what had to be done—*should have* been done—years and years ago. Though he doubted anyone would pin a medal on him, or want to invite him to a late-night talk show as a guest, he was convinced he was doing the right thing. He started the car, put it in gear, and drove off to his first appointment.

Juan Rodriguez wasn't in a good mood. Three of his "customers" hadn't shown up. He hadn't eaten supper and was starving. He was low on cash. And, to top it off, it was raining. All these things ran through his mind as he trudged down the rain-slick sidewalk. He hoped his last customer showed up on time.

Juan considered himself a businessman. He was meeting a need. He also hoped to move up the ladder—to enjoy some of the good life that money could buy—just like the men on the ladder above him. Money, fancy crib, fast cars, equally fast women—these were the perks Juan hoped would be his someday soon. Juan even dared to dream he would someday be the man on top of the ladder, with people like him and his bosses doing his bidding, satisfying his every whim. The fact that he was a low-level drug dealer didn't even cross Juan's mind.

The man followed Juan's progress down the street. He watched in disgust as this lowlife went on his way to sell his poison. Since his quarry was on a long, straight stretch, he started his car and drove to an intercept point at a side street. When he looked around the corner of the building he was hiding behind, he could see Juan approach. He waited until he was close, and stepped out onto the sidewalk. He didn't expect what happened next.

When Juan saw the black-clad figure, he turned and bolted. The man gave chase. He was in much better shape and would soon catch his prey. But Juan had a surprise up his sleeve. He reached behind him, under his shirt, and pulled out a chromed .32-caliber automatic. The man put on a burst of speed but Juan was able to elude him long enough to bring the pistol to bear. The man, however, wasn't without a surprise of his own. He reached around for his own nine-millimeter, in a holster in the small of his back. He wanted to wound Juan, but he had to rush his shot and caught Juan in the chest. He pitched forward, did a somersault, and lay inert on the sidewalk.

The man walked up to him, crouched, and felt for a pulse. To his dismay, Juan was dead.

He hadn't wanted it to end this way. Plus, there would be none of the desired information he sought this night. As he stood, the man was glad he had used a silencer. Not that he worried much about the police. They would probably write this off to a drive-by. The man headed back to his car, stooping to retrieve his expended cartridge. No sense giving the police any more help than necessary.

CHAPTER 2: LOVE AND MARRIAGE

Cilla sat at the dressing table, in her Philadelphia apartment, applying her minimal makeup. She hummed happily as she worked. Just then, her new husband, Vint, walked into the bedroom.

"Aren't you dressed yet?" Vint asked, "And must you *always* sit around the apartment without a stitch on?"

"Why not? I would think you'd enjoy seeing your newlywed wife in the altogether."

"I do, and I fully understand your reasons for it, but I'm just not used to seeing you naked so much. It's a lot to deal with all of a sudden, you know what I mean?"

Cilla looked up at Vint. "Does my being naked around you embarrass you, Honey?"

Vint could tell by the tone of her voice that Cilla wasn't kidding with him. "I didn't say it embarrasses me, it's just a whole lot different than the way I've lived all my life. In church we're taught that women should observe modesty and shouldn't dress provocatively."

"So you think my being naked is immodest and provocative?"

"No, not between us. It's just something I have to get used to."

Cilla stood up and stepped in front of Vint.

She took his hands in hers and looked up into his eyes. "So, it'll be okay then, if I'm naked around you all the time — as long as I'm modest and don't dress provocatively otherwise?"

Vint smiled down at her. "What am I supposed to say? Here you are, standing in the state of Eve, enticing me with your undraped form — I'm only human, after all."

"State of Eve? Undraped form? I love the anachronistic terms you use — like something out of an Emily Bronte novel. It was the first thing I noticed about you that first day in your office. You insisted on leaving the door open, remember?"

"Uh-huh. But I can't believe you think me anachronistic. And I doubt you've ever read an Emily Bronte novel."

"Oh yeah? I'll have you know I find Victorian literature quite erotic in its own way."

"You do, do you."

"Yes, all that smoldering sexuality couched in such evasive terms, it's a bit of a turn-on."

"I don't know whether to be flattered or insulted. So, I'm a sexy, Victorian kind of guy then?"

"Yes, and it's what I love about you. Now, if I can manage to coax you into the state of Adam...."

Vint looked down at his wife and answered her smile with one of his own. "You're incorrigible. I honestly don't know how I'm going to be able to deal with you once we get to exotic, erotic Miami. I think you're going to be quite a handful. How did I let you talk me into honeymooning there?"

"You let me *talk you into it* because you trust me — and it'll be fun," Cilla teased.

"You're probably right, but what do I do if you decide to go topless on South Beach?"

"Hey, I'm not twisting your arm, Sweetie."

"Don't get me wrong, I'm not backing out on this — but can we afford it?"

"Well, we're going to use my van and drive down. I also found an inexpensive motel in North Miami, away from the really expensive rates in Miami proper. The rooms have a refrigerator and hot plate, so we can cook and eat in. The funds are tight, but I think we can do it." Cilla began unbuttoning Vint's shirt.

"You know what I think about this penchant of yours for nakedness, right?"

Cilla turned her head up to look at Vint. "And *you* know why I have this 'penchant,' as you put it."

"But I would have thought being in that hole in the ground would have done just the opposite."

"Don't get me wrong — the being a captive part was terrifying. Being left in the dark — with literally nothing with which to protect myself, and nothing to do but think — I realized that being naked wasn't anything to fear. I was able to function in spite of it." Cilla took a deep breath and let it out in a rush. "I realized the way I dealt with it was under *my* control."

Vint studied Cilla's face. "Being in control means a lot to you, doesn't it?"

Cilla returned his gaze. "Yeah, I guess it does."

"Has it occurred to you that when you prayed to God in that hole, he helped you when you had *no* control?"

Cilla dropped her head. "Yes, it has," she said in a small voice.

"Good. I'm glad to hear you recognize that," Vint said, leaning forward to kiss the top of Cilla's head, "Now, about this 'state of Adam' thing...."

Printed in the United States
201646BV00001B/1-105/A